FAMOUS CLASSICS FOR GIRLS

HEIDI
WHAT KATY DID
BLACK BEAUTY

Retold and abridged for
younger readers

EGMONT

EGMONT

We bring stories to life

Famous Classics for Girls
First published in Great Britain 1963
by Golden Pleasure Books
This edition published 2011
by Egmont UK Limited
239 Kensington High Street
London W8 6SA

ISBN 978 1 4052 5466 3

1 3 5 7 9 10 8 6 4 2

A CIP catalogue record for this title is available from the British Library

Printed and bound in Spain

MIX
Paper
FSC FSC® C018306

Egmont is passionate about helping to preserve the world's remaining ancient forests. We only use paper from legal and sustainable forest sources, so we know where every single tree comes from that goes into every paper that makes up every book.

This book is made from paper certified by the Forestry Stewardship Council (FSC), an organisation dedicated to promoting responsible management of forest resources. For more information on the FSC, please visit **www.fsc.org**. To learn more about Egmont's sustainable paper policy, please visit **www.egmont.co.uk/ethical**.

HEIDI

by Johanna Spyri

When Aunt Dete went to work in Frankfurt she could not for the life of her think what to do with Heidi.

Heidi was only five, and what could you do with a little girl of five in a great city like Frankfurt? The trouble was that Heidi had no other family except Aunt Dete, for Heidi's mother and father died when she was a baby.

So there was no one in the world to look after her. No one? Yes, Dete suddenly remembered, there was Heidi's grandfather.

Dete hadn't seen him for years. Indeed few people had seen Heidi's grandfather of late.

He was a strange old man who lived the life of a hermit, all by himself halfway up the Alm Mountain in a wooden hut with only two goats for company. In the village below, the little Swiss village named Dörfli, they called him the 'Alm-Uncle', not because he was anybody's uncle, but just as a nickname.

No one, except young Peter the goatherd, ever saw or spoke to the Alm-Uncle. For he never came down to the village, even in winter when the mountain was covered in snow. He had quarrelled with everyone, even the parson. He was a cross and crotchety old man who hated everything except his pipe and his two goats and the tumble-down shack where he was content to live alone.

Dete, that bright June morning, was half afraid to go and see the Alm-Uncle, and she jerked at little Heidi's hand to get the unpleasant visit over as soon as possible.

But it was a long, steady climb up from Dörfli, up a steep mountain path, and they often had to stop to get their breath back. Heidi felt hot, for she was wearing all the clothes she owned, one dress over another, to save her aunt the trouble of carrying them. But she looked at the vast mountain and the smiling green valley which lay at her feet, and the green meadows around her with a thrill of delight.

She had not heard the people in Dörfli whispering as she and Dete started up the path. 'Poor little mite!' they said to each other. 'Imagine taking her up to the Alm-Uncle! Leaving her with that old ogre! It's a scandal, that's what it is. Dete ought to be ashamed of herself!'

Aunt Dete was a little ashamed of herself as she drew near the Alm-Uncle's poor hut. But what could she do? Hadn't she looked after the orphan child for four years? Now it was his turn to do something for Heidi. After all, he was her grandfather.

[8]

The old man was sitting on a wooden stool outside the hut when his visitors arrived, gloomily smoking his pipe. His unfriendly expression did not change when he saw them. He did not like to have his privacy disturbed.

Heidi, who reached the hut first, ran straight up to him and held out her hand.

'How do you do, grandfather,' she said.

'What's all this?' the old man asked roughly. And he stared at the little girl from beneath his bushy eyebrows.

Heidi stared back at him curiously, for she had never seen anyone like him. He had a long white beard and his thick eyebrows were like shaggy bushes. Then Dete came up, out of breath from the long climb.

'I've brought you Adelheid's child,' she said. Adelheid was the old man's dead daughter and Heidi's mother. 'You haven't seen her since she was a baby and now it's up to you to look after her.'

'But what can the child do here?' he growled. 'What can I do with her?'

'That's up to you,' said Dete rudely. 'Do what you please. But if any harm comes to her you will have to answer for it.'

The old man was so angry at the pert way she spoke to him that he rose from his stool and pointed to the path which led down the mountain.

'Go back where you came from,' he said sternly. 'And don't let me see you here again.'

Dete didn't have to be told twice.

'Goodbye then,' she said. 'And goodbye to you too, Heidi,' she added quickly and was gone, running down the path before either Heidi or the Alm-Uncle could say another word.

Dete didn't stop even when she reached Dörfli. She

didn't want to hear what the villagers would say about her for leaving poor Heidi with the strange old man of the mountain. Luckily by to-morrow she would be miles away in her fine new situation in Frankfurt.

* * * * *

When Dete had gone the Alm-Uncle went on puffing his pipe in silence. Heidi looked around. She went to the goats' shed nearby but it was empty. She found the fir trees behind the hut, and listened to the wind whispering high up in the branches.

Then she went into the hut. It had only one large room with a hayloft above it. There was a table, but only one chair. There was a fireplace where a kettle hung. In the cupboard there was cheese, a loaf of bread and a smoked ham. The old man's few clothes hung on a peg, and on a shelf stood a cup or two, some plates and simple cooking utensils. His bed stood in a corner.

And that was almost all. Everything the Alm-Uncle owned in the world — or needed — was in this one room.

'Where shall I sleep, grandfather?' she asked him.

'Where you like,' he said.

This suited Heidi. She climbed up into the hayloft where she found a heap of sweet-smelling hay and a small window through which she saw all the valley lying thousands of feet below.

'Come up, grandfather,' she called excitedly, 'and see how lovely it is.'

'I already know,' he said.

But he came up after a while and saw that Heidi had made a bed for herself in the soft fresh hay. And he brought

'I see you know how to be useful'

a blanket for her from his own bed and told her that she had made it very neatly.

'What do you say to something to eat?' he asked.

Heidi found that the cool mountain air had given her a tremendous appetite and she agreed eagerly. The old man fixed a piece of cheese on to an iron fork and began to toast it before the fire.

Before it was cooked Heidi had set the table with two bowls and two glasses, two knives and two forks. He looked at her slowly, then said:

'I see you know how to be useful. That's good.'

He filled her bowl full of fresh milk and when they had eaten he went into the shed beside the hut. There he made a little stool, exactly the right size for Heidi, who until now had not had anything to sit on. That afternoon Heidi followed him everywhere, interested in everything he did.

When evening came they heard a shrill whistle outside. Down from the mountain above them came Peter the goatherd with all the village goats that he took every day up into the high mountain meadows.

Two of them he left at the hut, for they belonged to Heidi's grandfather. One was white and one was brown. The white goat was called Swan and the brown one was called Bear. Heidi stroked them lovingly, hardly able to believe the good news that they were her grandfather's. They had their own shed which he kept neat and swept for them.

'Go and bring your bowl,' he said to Heidi, and when she obeyed he milked a goat into the bowl and gave it to her. With a huge piece of bread it made the nicest supper Heidi had ever eaten.

When she had said goodnight to her grandfather — and to Swan and Bear — she climbed up into the loft and went to bed. She fell asleep at once, lulled by the murmur of the wind in the tall fir trees outside.

But in the middle of the night her grandfather got up.

'Suppose,' he said to himself, 'the little girl is frightened.'

He climbed the ladder and in the moonbeams which came in through the little window he watched Heidi's face.

She was sleeping calmly and peacefully. Perhaps she was having sweet dreams, for there was a look of happiness on her face. He watched her for a long time, then quietly crept downstairs and went back to bed.

* * * * *

Early next morning Heidi was wakened by the same loud whistle she had heard yesterday evening. It was Peter, come for the goats.

Heidi jumped quickly out of bed and climbed down the ladder. Outside the hut stood Peter with his flock, and her grandfather was bringing Swan and Bear out of the shed to join the other goats.

'How would you like to go up to the pasture with them?' he asked her.

Heidi jumped for joy at the thought, but first her grandfather told her to wash in the big tub of cold water beside the door. She scrubbed herself so hard he had to laugh at her, for she looked as red and polished as a lobster. And he gave her a paper bag with so much cheese and bread in it that Peter's eyes were round with surprise.

The two children went merrily up the mountain slopes. The goats frisked around them, pausing often to nibble the rich green mountain grass. Everywhere the sky was bright blue and the early morning sun bathed everything in gold.

Heidi had never seen so many flowers — tender yellow primroses and clumps of pretty blue gentians. She picked them in handfuls and stuffed them into her apron to carry home to her grandfather.

She watched the goats playing together, leaping and enjoying themselves almost as much as Heidi did herself.

'Time to eat,' Peter said suddenly and he gave Heidi the bag which her grandfather had prepared.

For himself he kept a much smaller parcel, for Peter's family was poor and could not give him such a big dinner as Heidi's. When Heidi gave him the best part of her own dinner Peter was so amazed he almost forgot to say thank you.

[13]

The two children went merrily up the mountain

He told her the names of the different goats, for each goat had a name and a distinct personality. There was big Turk with his powerful horns who was always butting the others. There was little white Snowdrop who always bleated so pathetically that Heidi ran to her and put her arms around her neck to comfort her. There were many others, but Heidi thought the cleanest and prettiest of them all were Swan and Bear.

'Of course they are,' Peter agreed with her. 'That's because the Alm-Uncle takes such good care of them.'

And so the day passed until the sun went down behind the high mountain peak which was called the Falcon's Nest, because up there lived the robber-bird, high above the trees where no paths reached.

The setting sun turned everything red and glowing, as though the very mountain had caught fire. It was so beautiful that Heidi dreamed about it that night as she slept on her bed of sweet-smelling hay.

★   ★   ★   ★   ★

It grew colder as the days passed and one morning when the sun rose the whole mountainside was dazzling white. There was not a flower or green leaf to be seen. In the night the snow had silently covered everything.

Heidi helped her grandfather shovel the snow away from the front door and make paths out to the shed. It was great fun, and cosy afterwards sitting in front of the blazing fire.

Peter had not come up from the village for over a week, for the snow drifts were too deep. Later it froze harder and Peter was able to walk safely on the crust of the snow. He wanted Heidi to come down with him and visit his mother and grandmother who was old and blind. But how should Heidi make the journey?

Her grandfather came from the shed dragging behind him — a sled. He bundled Heidi up with blankets and took her in his lap where she was snug and warm. Then, guiding the sled with his right hand, he gave a push with his foot. Away shot the sled so swiftly that Heidi thought she was flying through the air like a bird. She laughed aloud with pleasure.

Almost before she knew it they reached the door of Peter's hut. Heidi went in by herself. In a corner of the little room sat an old woman bent over her spinning-wheel. She was

Heidi helped her grandfather shovel the snow away

blind and although she was really only Peter's grandmother everyone called her 'Granny'.

So Heidi did too. When Granny groped and found Heidi's outstretched hand she said:

'Peter's told me all about you. You are the little girl staying up with the Alm-Uncle. But don't tell me he actually brought you down himself!'

Heidi said that he had wrapped her up and brought her on his sled, and Granny was amazed that the old man had shown such kindness. Heidi told her how beautiful the snow was.

'Yes, my dear, I know,' the old woman nodded, 'though I cannot see it.'

So Heidi told her all about life in the Alm-Uncle's hut.

[16]

And Granny was again surprised to learn how good the old man had been to his granddaughter.

'God be praised,' she thought to herself. And when Heidi left her she kept saying to Peter and to Peter's mother: 'If only he'll let Heidi come to see me again.'

For it was the happiest afternoon the old blind woman had spent for many years.

Heidi did come again, many times that winter. And sometimes her grandfather came into the little house with her. He was very clever with hammer and nails and he helped make the draughty old house more comfortable for Peter's family who were very poor and had only ten-year-old Peter to look after them.

★ ★ ★ ★ ★

And so the winter passed and summer came. Two more summers went by quickly, too quickly, and Heidi was eight years old.

Heidi had learned much from living with her grandfather. She was useful around the house and could help make cheese as well as any grown-up. Swan and Bear followed her about like dogs, bleating with pleasure at the very sound of her voice.

But grandfather refused to let her go to school. He felt she could learn more from the wild life of the mountains than in the stuffy village below. And he could see how happy and healthy and pretty she had become.

Then one early spring morning they had a visitor. It was Dete, back from Frankfurt. Aunt Dete looked very smart in her fashionable new clothes, but Heidi's grandfather looked her over without saying a word.

Aunt Dete began to talk about Frankfurt

Aunt Dete began to talk about Frankfurt and how fine it was to live in a great city. Grandfather's face became even more stern and harsh.

Finally Aunt Dete came to the reason for her unexpected visit. Some rich relations of the woman for whom Aunt Dete worked were looking for a companion for their daughter. Their daughter was lame and spent her life in a wheel-chair. She was always alone and needed someone to do her lessons with.

They wanted an unspoiled child to be the little lame girl's playmate. Dete said she had at once thought of Heidi. They were very rich and it seemed a wonderful opportunity. Such luck for Heidi ...

'Will you never finish?' the old man interrupted angrily.

Then Dete began to reproach him for his selfishness. He had no right to spoil the child's life. Besides she, Dete, had just as much to say about Heidi's future as he did.

'Be quiet!' shouted the old man. 'She can do what she likes. But if she ever comes into this house all dressed up like you I'll slam the door in her face.'

And he marched out of the room.

'You've upset my grandfather,' Heidi said crossly and began to follow him.

But Dete stopped her. 'He'll come to his senses,' she said. 'Now get your things together and come with me.'

'No, I won't,' said Heidi.

Dete paid no attention to her, but bundled her into her hat and coat. She kept telling Heidi how lovely Frankfurt was and how happy grandfather would be when Heidi came back again, a fine lady.

'Can I come back again to-night?' Heidi asked.

'Whenever you want to,' Dete nodded, hurrying her out of the hut and down the path.

Dete led her through Dörfli so fast that Heidi couldn't even say goodbye to Peter and Granny. Dete said she could bring Granny back something nice from Frankfurt, if Heidi made haste.

When the villagers saw Heidi and Dete hurrying down towards the railway station they said to each other: 'The poor little girl is running away from the Alm-Uncle and I don't blame her! Yet what rosy cheeks she has.'

From the day Heidi left the Alm Mountain her grandfather grew more and more ill-natured and grumpy. He spoke to no one and everyone avoided him.

[19]

The villagers saw Heidi and Dete hurrying towards the station

Only blind Granny took his part, saying how kind and good he had been. And to her daughter and Peter she often said with a sigh: 'How empty our days seem now that Heidi has gone. May the good Lord grant that I hear her voice once more before I die.'

In the beautiful great house in Frankfurt a little lame girl sat in her wheel-chair. Her name was Klara Sesemann and she was waiting with great excitement for the arrival of her new little companion from the mountains in far away Switzerland.

'Isn't it time yet, Fräulein Rottenmeier?' she kept asking her governess.

Fräulein Rottenmeier was a stiff, humourless old maid

Heidi's appearance did not please Fräulein Rottenmeier

who ruled the house with a rod of iron. At least she did when Herr Sesemann, Klara's father, was away on business. Klara's mother was dead and so the governess bossed everybody, including the cook, the housemaid, Sebastian the butler, and all the other servants.

Heidi's appearance did not please Fräulein Rottenmeier. She looked at the little girl's plain cotton dress and old straw hat with disapproval.

'What is your name?' she asked coldly.

'Heidi.'

'What a very funny name,' Fräulein Rottenmeier sniffed. 'How old are you?'

'Eight,' said Heidi.

[21]

'Four years too young,' said the old maid. 'Klara is twelve. What books have you studied?'

'None.'

'None?' She was shocked. 'How did you learn to read then?'

'I can't read. Neither can Peter.'

Fräulein Rottenmeier was horrified. 'Then what have you learned?'

'Nothing,' said Heidi truthfully.

Fräulein Rottenmeier left the room with Dete to say that this savage little girl would not do at all. Alone with Heidi Klara said to her:

'I don't think Heidi is a funny name. I like it. And my tutor will quickly teach you to read. It's easy. I'm glad you've come.'

Meanwhile Heidi's simple belongings had been taken up to the room which the servants had made ready for her. Fräulein Rottenmeier, thinking to get rid of Heidi next day, gave orders for supper to be served.

Sebastian, the butler, waited on them at table. Next to Heidi's plate there was a lovely soft white roll. She looked at it enviously and whispered to Sebastian:

'Can I have that?'

Sebastian hid a smile and nodded. He almost laughed out loud when he saw Heidi slip the roll quickly into her pocket.

When supper was finished Fräulein Rottenmeier spoke to Heidi with a sigh. 'I see I shall have to teach you table manners,' she said. 'In the first place, you are not to speak to the servants, except to give them orders. Then . . .'

Fräulein Rottenmeier's instructions went on and on. Heidi tried hard to listen but it had been a long day. At last the governess broke off in annoyance.

[22]

'I don't think Heidi is a funny name'

But Klara only smiled.

'Heidi's been asleep for the past ten minutes!' she exclaimed.

★ ★ ★ ★ ★

Her first day in Frankfurt was a strange day for Heidi, but even stranger for Fräulein Rottenmeier.

At first Heidi couldn't think where she was. When she woke up and jumped from the big white bed and ran to the long velvet curtains at the window she didn't see green meadows and the snow on high mountains, nor the little stream winding through the valley below. All she saw was brick walls and houses. There was no sunshine and no sound

[23]

of the wind in the fir trees—only the sound of carriages rattling over the stone streets outside.

Heidi felt as though she had been locked up in a cage. But if Heidi felt she was in a cage poor Fräulein Rottenmeier felt that she herself was locked up with a strange, savage animal.

The child know nothing of how to behave in a great, well-run household. She was late to meals. Her clothes were not correct. She made friends with the servants. She was hopeless when it came to lesson time.

* * * * *

But Klara had become much more cheerful since Heidi's arrival. She liked talking to Heidi about life in the mountains, about Swan and Bear and the other goats, about Peter and Heidi's grandfather. For Klara the next few days were much less dull than usual.

Heidi was less happy. To-morrow, she kept thinking, I really must go home. But one thing pleased her. Every day she took more rolls from the table and hid them in her room. She was saving them for Granny. Granny's teeth were no longer able to chew the hard, black bread which was all she had, and Heidi planned to take back to her the lovely soft rolls for a present.

At last one day she wrapped them all up in her red shawl, put on her old straw hat and started for home. But at the door she met Fräulein Rottenmeier.

'Where are you going? I have strictly forbidden you to wander about the streets by yourself!' Fräulein Rottenmeier said angrily. 'And in that shabby old hat! And what—what are you doing with all those rolls?'

[24]

'Where are you going?'

'I'm only going home,' said Heidi. 'I've been away too long. Swan and Bear must be missing me and . . .'

'Good gracious!' exclaimed the governess. 'The child is mad!' And she called in alarm for Sebastian, ordering him to lock Heidi up in her room.

For Fräulein Rottenmeier was really worried. It was not that she cared whether Heidi was homesick and miserable, but Herr Sesemann, Klara's father, was expected. And what would Herr Sesemann say if he thought that poor Heidi had been driven from his house by Fräulein Rottenmeier's unkindness?

* * * * * *

Herr Sesemann arrived the very next day, bringing heaps of presents for his lame daughter and others for Klara's new companion. For Klara and Heidi it was like Christmas. Everyone liked Herr Sesemann, and Fräulein Rottenmeier was a little in awe of him.

She at once told him how unsatisfactory Heidi was, but he only smiled at her, and gave instructions that Heidi was to be treated exactly like his own daughter Klara. Herr Sesemann was a man of the world and he understood people well. He liked Heidi at first sight. Besides, he knew that Klara loved her already.

The nicest thing that Herr Sesemann brought home with him was the news that his mother, Lady Sesemann, was to pay them a visit. She was Klara's grandmother and such a grand old lady that the whole house was thrown into an uproar by preparations for her arrival. Fräulein Rottenmeier spent half the day telling Heidi how to behave in the presence of her ladyship, so that Heidi was half-frightened when the big carriage finally rolled up to the door.

But Lady Sesemann turned out to be much less frightening than Fräulein Rottenmeier was herself. She took to Heidi, just as her son had done, and that afternoon she showed Heidi a lovely book she had brought with her.

'What good is it to show a book to her?' Fräulein Rottenmeier wanted to know. 'The stupid child can't even read.'

'Is that true, my dear?' Lady Sesemann asked Heidi kindly.

'Yes,' Heidi said. 'The tutor has tried to teach me, but it's too hard. Peter has tried to learn and he says it can't be done.'

'Now, Heidi,' Klara's grandmother said, making Heidi sit down beside her, 'I'll tell you something. You can't read, because you believed Peter. Now I want you to believe me.

That afternoon, she showed Heidi a lovely book

You are not a stupid child and I know you can learn, and quite quickly too.'

And she showed Heidi the beautiful pictures which the book contained. One picture was so lovely that it brought tears to Heidi's eyes. It was a picture of a shepherd, standing in a green meadow. Around him browsed sheep and goats.

'Come, don't cry,' Lady Sesemann said gently. 'The picture made you think of your home, but soon you will be able to read the story and that will make you very happy. Tell me, what's the matter?'

But Heidi couldn't tell her. Ever since Fräulein Rottenmeier had scolded her for trying to run away she had felt ashamed of seeming ungrateful to the Sesemanns who were so kind to her.

'But you mustn't go home, Heidi,' said Klara

So she said nothing. But every day her heart felt heavier. She ate less and less and grew pale.

'Tell me, my dear, what is the matter with you?' the old lady often begged.

'I cannot tell anyone,' Heidi said, and she looked so unhappy that Klara's grandmother was sorry for her.

And she told Heidi that there was someone to whom she could tell everything. She could tell our dear Lord and He would help her. That night before she went to sleep Heidi knelt beside her bed and prayed to the Lord that she might be allowed to go home...

A week passed. One morning the tutor came in high spirits to Lady Sesemann to report a wonderful happening.

Heidi could read!

That evening at the supper table Heidi found the beautiful picture-book lying beside her plate. She saw Lady Sesemann smiling at her.

'Yes, child,' she said. 'Now it belongs to you.'

'For always?' Heidi said, going pink with pleasure. 'Even when I go home?'

'For always. Of course.'

'But you mustn't go home, Heidi,' said Klara. 'Please, please stay with me.'

* * * * *

The day came when Lady Sesemann's visit drew near an end. Everyone—except Fräulein Rottenmeier—was very sad at the thought, especially Heidi who had learned to love the old lady more and more. She had taught Heidi to sew—she made sewing seem like a kind of game—and that afternoon she asked suddenly:

'Do you still tell all your troubles to the Lord, my dear child?'

'No,' said Heidi. 'Because it's no use. I did, but He didn't listen. I suppose it's because He has so many other people to listen to.'

Then Klara's grandmother told Heidi that He certainly listened to her, as He listens to everyone who prays to Him. He only forgets those who forget Him.

'And remember, Heidi,' she said, 'He knows better what is good for us than we do ourselves. Perhaps He is saying to Himself: "Yes, Heidi shall have what she asks for, but not until it is good for her to have it." You see, He wants us to trust Him, and to realise that He knows best when to grant us our prayers.'

Heidi tried to understand this, and that night she prayed again that she might be allowed to go home.

The Sesemann house seemed empty and sad when the old lady finally left. But Heidi found pleasure in reading aloud to her friend Klara.

So many days passed. Weeks became months and summer became winter. Inside the walls of the Sesemann house every season seemed the same to Heidi. And she wondered whether the Alm Mountain was covered with shimmering snow, or whether the meadows were bright with bluebells and rock-roses for the goats to frisk among. Every day Heidi grew more homesick.

Then one day Fräulein Rottenmeier discovered that the house was haunted! No one had actually seen the ghost, but it always left the front door open in the middle of the night. The servants were all afraid to go to sleep at night and even Sebastian carefully locked and bolted his own door before going to bed.

Fräulein Rottenmeier wrote in panic to Herr Sesemann who had gone to Paris on business. She begged him to come home at once for fear the ghost should terrify his poor, lame daughter. Actually Klara was not nearly so terrified as Fräulein Rottenmeier was herself, but Herr Sesemann, fearing for his daughter's health, came back to Frankfurt on the first train.

He didn't believe in ghosts, but he thought there might be thieves around who entered the house at night.

So he got his friend the doctor to sit up with him all night in the library, waiting for the ghostly visitor. Both men were armed with revolvers, and as midnight came they sat in silence, feeling a little nervous.

'Don't you like being in Frankfurt?'

Twelve o'clock struck, but there was no sound. Surely it must be a thief and they had scared him away. Half past twelve struck, then one o'clock. They were about to laugh when the doctor raised a finger in warning.

'Sshh . . . I think I heard something,' he whispered.

It was at the front door—the sound of a bolt being slid back, then the sound of the key turning in the lock!

The two men grasped their revolvers and tiptoed forward. Their hearts were beating faster now.

The front door was wide open. There in the pale moonlight stood a motionless white figure.

'Who is there?' the doctor shouted.

The white figure began to tremble. It spun round with

a little cry. It was Heidi in her bare feet and wearing nothing but her nightdress.

She had been walking in her sleep.

'This is a case for me,' the doctor said to Herr Sesemann.

He lifted up Heidi in his arms, telling her not to be afraid. He took her up to her room again and held her until she stopped shivering. Then he tucked her up in bed and said soothingly:

'There now. There's nothing to worry about, my dear. But would you like to tell me where you were going?'

'I don't know,' Heidi said, for she could remember nothing at all about it. 'I was dreaming, I think. Every night I dream and always the same thing.'

'Tell me, child,' he said gently.

'I dream I'm at home with my grandfather and the fir trees are whispering to me and the stars are sparkling above the mountain. It is so very beautiful. But when I wake up I'm always in Frankfurt.'

'Don't you like being in Frankfurt?'

'Yes,' she said, but so faintly that the doctor knew she was only trying to be polite.

'Isn't it very cold and uncomfortable in the hut up in the mountains?'

'Oh no!' Heidi said. 'It is the loveliest place in the whole world.'

The doctor smoothed her pillow and rose.

'Cry a little, if you want to,' he said softly. 'It won't hurt you. Then to-morrow you'll find that everything is all right.'

And he went softly out of the room. In the library down-stairs he spoke to Herr Sesemann gravely.

'The poor little child,' he said, 'is suffering from acute

[32]

homesickness. That's why she walks in her sleep. She is also so thin and wasted that she may soon fall dangerously ill.'

'Then what shall we do?' asked Herr Sesemann in alarm. 'Give her everything she needs, any treatment that is necessary. As you know, no expense must be spared.'

'There is only one thing she needs,' said the doctor. 'There is only one treatment which can save her. She must be sent back to the Alm Mountain. She must go home—at once.'

* * * * *

Sebastian had been told to take her all the way to Dörfli. They travelled all day in a train and spent the night in Basle where Herr Sesemann had reserved a room for them in an hotel. Next morning they travelled again and at noon got out at the little station below Dörfli.

Dörfli was in the mountains, though not so high up as the Alm-Uncle's lonely hut, and Sebastian looked at the narrow, twisting mountain road with nervous doubt. To him the road didn't look safe. He was glad when a villager with a waggon promised to take Heidi up to the village, though he was sorry to say goodbye to the little girl.

Heidi, holding tight to the basket which contained white rolls for Granny, looked around eagerly. Her heart raced with excitement.

'You're the child who lived up with the Alm-Uncle, aren't you?' the man in the waggon said. 'Did they treat you so badly in Frankfurt that you decided to run home again?'

'No. Herr Sesemann was very kind to me,' Heidi said. 'But I'd rather live with my grandfather than with anybody else.'

'You may change your mind when you get there,' the man said.

[33]

But Heidi didn't. She was gazing at the high peaks. The Falcon's Nest seemed to look down and greet her like an old friend. Heidi wanted to jump from the waggon and run towards it.

They reached Dörfli as the church clock was striking five and she began to run towards the steep path which led up the mountain. How well she remembered it, every rock and tree, every bend and turn. Her heart beat faster and faster.

On the way she passed Peter's tumble-down house.

She opened the door, hardly daring to breathe. She ran into the middle of the room, trembling. A voice sounded from a dark corner.

'Dear me,' it said, 'our little Heidi used to run in like that! Who is it?'

'It's me,' cried Heidi, and she rushed to the corner.

Granny was there, just as she'd always been! Heidi threw her arms around her. Granny felt Heidi's curly hair, stroking it with shaking fingers.

'Yes, it's Heidi's hair,' she murmured. 'And it's Heidi's voice. May the dear Lord be thanked for this moment!' Two tears ran from her blind old eyes and splashed on to Heidi's hand.

'Don't cry, Granny,' Heidi begged. 'See what I've brought you.' And she piled all the rolls into Granny's lap.

Peter's mother came in and exclaimed with astonishment at finding Heidi there. Peter's mother was especially surprised and delighted with Heidi's fine silk dress and new hat, trimmed with ostrich feathers. Heidi gave her the splendid hat at once. She took off the silk dress and put on the old red shawl and battered straw hat she always used to wear. Grandfather, she thought, wouldn't recognise her in anything else.

'And now I must go and find him,' she said.

[34]

She could only throw herself into his arms

The Falcon's Nest was aflame with the glory of sunset when Heidi climbed the steep mountain path. Never, even in her dreams, had the mountain been more lovely. Tears of joy and gratitude ran down her cheeks. She could not find words to express her happiness and thankfulness to the dear Lord to whom she had so often prayed — just for this.

Then she saw *him* — on the little wooden stool, smoking his pipe as usual; she saw her grandfather. She couldn't say a word. She could only throw herself into his arms and cling to his neck. For a long time Grandfather, too, could think of nothing to say. He just held onto her.

'I didn't know you would come back,' he said at last. 'Now come and get your milk.'

Heidi gave him a parcel Herr Sesemann had sent. But Grandfather put it in the cupboard and said that it belonged to Heidi. It was money.

That night Heidi slept in the hayloft on her bed of sweet-smelling hay to the music of the wind in the fir trees. She slept better than she had for a long, long time.

But during the night her grandfather climbed the ladder up to the hayloft at least ten times to make sure that she was really there.

* * * * *

The next day was Saturday and in the afternoon the Alm-Uncle walked down to Peter's house with Heidi. Heidi could hardly wait to see Granny again and hear how the rolls had tasted.

Peter's mother told her how Granny enjoyed them.

Then Heidi found Granny's old hymn-book, covered with dust for Granny had not been able to see it for many years. Heidi opened it and began to read. She read to Granny those hymns which the old lady had not heard for so long. Granny's face lightened with joy as she heard the old, familiar words read so clearly in Heidi's sweet young voice.

That night after supper in the mountain hut Heidi said to her grandfather:

'How wise the dear Lord was not to grant my wishes too soon! For if He had let me come home when I first prayed to come home I shouldn't have been able to bring Granny all those rolls. And I shouldn't have been able to read to her. Klara's grandmother told me that He knows what is good for us better than we know ourselves. And she was right. He never forgets us, Grandfather.'

[36]

Heidi opened it and began to read

'Sometimes I think He does,' the old man grumbled.

'No, never,' Heidi said. 'Klara's grandmother said so. She said He only forgets us when we forget Him.'

Her grandfather was silent at this. Afterwards he asked Heidi to read to him from the lovely book Klara's grandmother had given to her. Heidi read to him the story of the Prodigal Son — who had come back to ask his father's forgiveness and been welcomed home with joy.

Long after Heidi had gone to bed that night the sour old man sat thinking about the story she had read him. Just before he went to bed himself he folded his hands and bowed his head.

'Father,' he said, half-aloud, 'Father, I too have sinned

against You and my fellow men, and no longer am worthy to be called Thy Son . . .'

Tears rolled down his rough old cheeks, the first tears he had shed for many long years.

The sun rose bright and golden next morning.

'Wake up, Heidi!' Grandfather called in a cheerful voice. 'It's Sunday. Put on your best new dress. We're going to church together!'

The Alm-Uncle in church! No one in Dörfli had ever heard of such a thing! Everyone nudged his neighbour and glanced at him as he sat, bolt upright, in the pew beside his little granddaughter. Heidi thought she had never seen her grandfather looking so well as he did that morning in his carefully brushed Sunday coat with its polished silver buttons.

The parson preached a specially fine sermon that Sunday. He too was pleased to see such a stranger in the congregation. The last time he had met the Alm-Uncle the old man had been quarrelsome and rude, bitterly refusing to allow Heidi to come down to the village school.

The parson was even more pleased when, after the service, the Alm-Uncle came to his study door. He took the old man's hand in his and shook it warmly.

'I've come to ask you to forget my words when we last met,' said the Alm-Uncle. 'You were right when you said Heidi ought to go to school. Next winter we shall come down to Dörfli and live among our neighbours.'

The parson smiled with pleasure. 'We shall all welcome you among us again,' he said. 'And I hope you will spend many hours before my fireplace. For it would give me great joy to talk to you and be your friend.'

[38]

The Alm-Uncle in church! No one had ever heard of such a thing

Everyone in Dörfli crowded round the Alm-Uncle when he came out again from the parson's study. Everyone wanted to shake his hand. It seemed suddenly that the Alm-Uncle had become the most popular person in the village.

*   *   *   *   *

'Grandfather,' said Heidi, 'I've never seen you looking so handsome before. Is it the coat?'

'No, Heidi.' His eyes twinkled. 'It's because I feel on good terms with people and at peace with God and man.' He paused outside Peter's house to say good-day to Granny, and to ask if there were any repairs or carpentry he could do.

Peter arrived with a letter

Granny was overjoyed at his visit. 'May God reward you,' she exclaimed.

'He already has,' the Alm-Uncle smiled. 'He has sent Heidi back to me. In fact He has sent Heidi back to all of us.'

Peter arrived, breathless, a few minutes later. He had a letter which had been given to him at the post office in Dörfli. It was addressed to Heidi and it was from Klara Sesemann.

Klara wrote that the big house in Frankfurt had been silent and dreary since Heidi left. She wrote that she had been so lonely that her father had promised her she could come to visit Heidi in Dörfli. Lady Sesemann too was going to come along. Lady Sesemann sent word that Heidi had done quite the right thing in bringing the rolls to Granny. She was sending a bag of coffee at once so that Granny could have some coffee to go with them.

When were they coming? Not until the middle of September, Klara said.

What Klara didn't say—for she didn't know it herself—was that the doctor didn't think Klara was well enough to travel and wouldn't be until September, if then.

The doctor called on Herr Sesemann early one September morning on a sad errand. He had come to say that Klara was still too ill to take the long trip to Switzerland.

Another sorrow had recently come into the doctor's life; he had lost his own daughter. The doctor's wife had died some years before and his only child had been all that made life worth while to him. He didn't want his friend Herr Sesemann to suffer as he did.

The two men went together to see Klara. Klara tried hard not to cry when she learned she couldn't go, and she suddenly had an idea.

'Why don't you go yourself, doctor?' she exclaimed. 'You can take things to Heidi from me. Then afterwards you can come back and tell me all about her '

And so, when the middle of September came around, Dörfli had a visitor from Frankfurt after all—though it wasn't poor Klara.

* * * * *

The day when Heidi expected her visitors from Frankfurt dawned blue and gold. The Alm Mountain had never looked more beautiful. Peter came early with his herd of goats. They played cheerfully in the fresh air which already had a touch

[41]

She took him by the hand and led him up towards the hut

of autumn in it. They, too, seemed to know that to-day was somehow a special day.

Heidi was up even before the sun. Peter was disappointed when she said she could not come up to the meadows with him that day. Perhaps he was a little jealous of the fine friends from the big city that she was expecting.

Heidi spent the whole morning sweeping and polishing the hut. Her grandfather was pleased that she had become such a good housekeeper. She kept the place as though every day was Sunday, he said.

To-day she kept running to the front door to admire the view over the mountains, to watch the fir trees sway in the brisk breeze which came up from the valley, or to listen to the birds chattering under the eaves. But her grandfather knew she was really waiting for her friends to appear on the path below. At last he heard her excited cry:

'They're coming, Grandfather, they're coming. The doctor has come with them.'

She rushed down to meet him, her face alight with joy. The doctor was a little surprised by the warmth of his welcome. He hadn't expected the child even to remember him. He didn't know that Heidi would always remember that night when he had taken her up in his arms and comforted her and told her to cry a little and that to-morrow everything would be all right. Heidi believed she owed her home-coming to the doctor.

'But where are the others?' Heidi asked. 'Klara and her grandmother?'

The doctor saw the disappointment in her face when he had to explain that Klara couldn't come.

'Perhaps in the spring,' he said, 'when the days are longer and warmer. I'm sorry to bring you bad news.'

And he looked as upset as Heidi was herself. He was thinking of his own dead daughter and of how much he had always hated to disappoint her. Heidi saw the pain in his eyes. He looked sadder than she had ever seen him before, and she tried to think of something cheerful to say to him.

'Spring won't be long,' she smiled. 'With us time goes quickly. But I'm very glad you came, Doctor. Grandfather will be glad to see you too.'

She took him by the hand and led him up towards the hut. The doctor, who had been wrapped in his own thoughts, suddenly opened his eyes and saw how beautiful the scenery around him was. He had only meant to stay a day in Dörfli,

[43]

but now he wondered if a longer stay might not be possible.

Grandfather greeted him with a hearty shake of the hand. Heidi had talked so much about the doctor that he felt he already knew him. He apologised because he could not invite the doctor to sleep in the tiny hut, but urged him to stay for dinner. Afterwards they would go down and find a room at the inn.

Heidi laid the table in front of the hut The brisk mountain air had sharpened the doctor's appetite and he said he had never enjoyed a dinner so much.

When they had finished they saw a porter coming slowly up the path with a heavy trunk on his back. It was the box from Klara which the doctor had brought in the train from Frankfurt.

What fun it was unpacking it! There was a present for everybody: tobacco for Grandfather, cakes and sausages for Peter's family, a large woollen shawl for Granny. There were dozens of things for Heidi too. The doctor laughed aloud with pleasure as he saw the little girl's black eyes dance.

'And what is the nicest thing I've brought from Frankfurt?' he asked her.

Heidi stopped to consider the question. What gave her most pleasure of all the things that had come from Frankfurt? She answered the doctor's question quite honestly.

'Yourself,' she said.

* * * * *

The doctor stayed in Dörfli all the rest of September. His visit was a great success. The presents he had brought delighted everyone, but perhaps Heidi was right when she said the nicest thing he'd brought was himself.

Only Peter was not so sure he liked the doctor's being there. For the older man took up much of Heidi's time, often coming with them into the high mountains where the goats grazed. But the sausages made up for it. Peter had never seen such huge sausages or so many at one time. His eyes nearly popped out of his head when they were brought down to his house.

Granny was delighted with the shawl. Though she couldn't see it she could feel it—and it was the softest, warmest thing she had ever known. It made the cold weather almost worth looking forward to!

Often the doctor went on long mountain excursions with Grandfather. The Alm-Uncle knew the mounatins better than anyone in the village. He knew where the rarest plants grew and he was familiar with all the lesser-known paths and byways. The two men became close friends.

When the day came for him to go back to Frankfurt everyone was sad, even Peter. Heidi walked halfway down the valley with him. He held her hand in his, but for the first time they found nothing to say to each other. The doctor was thinking how swiftly the days had passed.

Finally he stopped and said that Heidi had come far enough with him. He tried to look cheerful as he patted her curly head and again asked her to thank the Alm-Uncle for all his kindness.

'Now I must say goodbye,' he sighed. 'If only I could take you back to Frankfurt with me, Heidi!'

Heidi thought of Frankfurt and of its dreary stone streets, its rows of houses and stuffy rooms. She said, somewhat shyly:

'It would be much nicer if you came back here instead.'

[45]

'Now I must say goodbye'

'Yes, of course it would,' the doctor said quickly. For he knew that he had been dreaming of something impossible. He had already seen what happened to Heidi in the city. 'I was only joking,' he said.

But he didn't sound as though he was joking. Heidi saw that his kind eyes had grown misty as though with tears. He turned away quickly and hurried down the path. Heidi watched him and her heart turned over with a sympathy she did not altogether understand.

'Doctor,' she called after him. 'If you really want me to I will come to Frankfurt with you. Only I must go back first and tell Grandfather.'

The doctor smiled. 'No, my dear,' he murmured. 'But thank you just the same. Someday perhaps . . .'

[46]

He didn't finish the sentence. He was gone before Heidi could say goodbye.

★　★　★　★　★

Towards the end of October the first snows fell on the Alm Mountain. The Alm-Uncle remembered the promise he had made to the parson and he came down from the mountain to live in the village near the school where Heidi was now enrolled as a pupil.

They found a large old deserted house which was all draughts and had no windows, but the Alm-Uncle quickly boarded everything up until the place was nearly as snug as the hut.

Heidi had a small bed in a nook behind the great stove where she slept comfortably enough, though at first she missed the fragrant hayloft and the sound of the wind in the fir trees at night. Grandfarher, too, missed the loneliness of the high alpine meadows for a day or two, but the parson and the other men in Dörfli soon made him feel at home. Even Swan and Bear settled down after a while in the warm stalls which Grandfather built for them in an empty part of the old house.

After the heavy snows fell Heidi didn't see much of Peter and Peter's family who lived halfway up the path towards the hut. The soft snow was so deep that Peter had to dig his way out of the window to reach the road. He used this as an excuse for not going to school. For Peter hated school.

At last the soft snow froze into a hard crust and travelling was easier. Peter managed to come down to see Heidi, even if he didn't get so far as the school-house! He came down on his sled, shooting like lightning over the sparkling snow. He told his mother he was going to school, but he didn't go.

[47]

The Alm-Uncle knew quite well that Peter was playing truant when the boy called at their new winter house. He'd once been a boy himself.

'What would you do with a goat that kept wandering off?' he asked the lad.

'Beat him,' replied Peter promptly.

'And if a boy behaved exactly like a goat?'

Then Peter understood what the old man meant, and he blushed. For the Alm-Uncle was the only man Peter really respected. He decided to go to school the very next day.

Meanwhile the Alm-Uncle asked him to stay to dinner. Afterwards he could take Heidi over the hard snow to see Granny again. It was the first time for weeks.

Peter and Heidi had lots to talk about—the new house, Heidi's adventures in school, how Swan and Bear were liking their new winter barn.

Heidi spent the afternoon reading aloud from Granny's hymn-book, those old, familiar hymns which brought such light and comfort to the old woman's heart. It grew so late as she read that night had fallen before she went.

But outside the full moon shed its radiance over the snow-covered world. It was almost as bright and clear as day time. Peter had his sled ready and they raced down to the village.

Heidi thought a lot about Granny before she went to sleep that night. If only there was some way to see her more often and read to her. Being read aloud to was what gave her such pleasure.

Just before she dropped off to sleep. Heidi had an idea. The idea was so simple she wondered why she had not thought of it before: Peter should learn to read.

* * * * *

[48]

They raced down to the village

So poor Peter began to go to school much more regularly. He didn't like it, but he was afraid of what the Alm-Uncle would say if he didn't. And Heidi, too, made sure that he missed no more classes.

'Of course you can learn to read,' she told him.

'Can't,' he said.

'I'll teach you with my book, the way Klara's grandmother taught me. It's fun. Then every day you can read hymns to Granny.'

'Don't want to,' he grumbled.

But Heidi only laughed at him and began on the A-B-C. It cannot be said that Peter was a good pupil, but Heidi kept on at him all the winter. Even the schoolmaster was surprised.

But no one was as surprised as Peter's mother when one evening towards the end of winter he came rushing in.

'I can do it,' he shouted.

'Do what?' his mother wondered.

'Read,' he said. 'Now I'll read Granny a hymn.'

And he sat down at the table and began.

He didn't read very well. He stumbled over all the long words, but his mother thought he was wonderful. Granny was amused at his trying so hard and she thanked him politely, though in secret she thought the hymns sounded quite different and much more beautiful when Heidi read them.

* * * * *

In spring, Heidi and her grandfather moved up to their hut on the mountain again. Heidi ran everywhere, re-visiting all her favourite spots. She was as gay as the birds which nested in the woods, and she leapt like the goats themselves for the very joy of being alive.

In the workshop behind the hut her grandfather was busy sawing and hammering. He had already made a splendid new stool to sit on and was starting on another. They were for Klara and Klara's grandmother.

'Do you think,' Heidi asked, a little nervously, 'that Fräulein Rottenmeier will come too?'

Grandfather gave her the letter which had just come up from Dörfli. It was from Klara. This time, Klara wrote, all was well. The doctor himself was actually urging her to come to Dörfli. Everything was already packed, and Grandmother was coming too.

But, Klara wrote, Fräulein Rottenmeier refused to come.

She saw the strange procession winding its way up the path

Sebastian had given her such a terrifying description of the mountain and its dangers that she was too frightened to move from Frankfurt.

Heidi ran down to tell Granny the wonderful news. Granny tried to share the little girl's pleasure, but inside she was worried—worried that Heidi's rich friends would carry her away again Peter, when he heard that strangers were expected, was cross and jealous.

Heidi didn't guess this. She was too happy at the thought of seeing her dear friends.

Then one warm morning in June she saw the strange procession winding its way up the path. First came two men carrying a chair in which a lame girl sat wrapped in shawls and blankets. Then came a grand old lady on a fine horse. Then an empty wheel-chair, pushed by a servant. And finally a porter with shawls, blankets, furs and rugs.

Heidi almost tumbled down the hill in her eagerness to meet them. Klara, in her chair, looked weak but very glad to see Heidi again. Lady Sesemann got down from her horse and took Heidi in her arms. Then she turned to greet Heidi's grandfather, calling him Alm-Uncle, the way everyone in Dörfli did and as though she had known him all her life. Indeed she had heard so much about him from the doctor that she felt she had.

Klara fell in love with everything she saw. She gazed around her, enchanted. It was even more lovely than Heidi had said it was. The Alm-Uncle put her in her wheel-chair, wrapped her cosily in rugs, and pushed her out where she could see the view better. Years ago, in the army, he had been a medical orderly, and knew well how to look after the sick.

'The flowers!' cried Klara. 'Whole fields of bluebells! Oh, if I could only run and pick them!'

Heidi ran and picked them for her, while her grandfather toasted some of the cheese he himself made from the goats' milk. Klara ate it as she had never eaten before.

'Oh, grandmama, it's so good!' she cried.

'It's our mountain air,' the Alm-Uncle laughed. 'Not the cook!'

The afternoon passed too quickly for them all. Even Lady Sesemann was surprised to see the sun already sinking. They were staying down in the village in the inn.

'I'm afraid,' she said, 'it's time for us to go, Klara my dear.'

'Oh, just a little longer,' Klara pleaded.

The Alm-Uncle drew Klara's grandmother aside and

spoke so that the children couldn't hear. 'Why not,' he said, 'let Klara stay with us? There's plenty of room for her to sleep beside Heidi in the hayloft. And I can look after them both.'

Lady Sesemann hesitated only for a second. Then she grasped the old man's hand. 'That's a wonderful idea!' she said. 'And I thank you with all my heart.'

So Klara, too, stayed in the mountain hut. At dusk she saw Peter returning with his herd and met Swan and Bear whom she had heard so much about. And she drank their milk, fresh and foaming, and even asked for a second bowl.

That night she slept beside Heidi and looked out through the little window where the vast blue-black sky was shimmering with stars. She slept better than she had ever slept in her life, and she dreamed of the Falcon's Nest, of flower-strewn meadows and bright twinkling stars.

★　★　★　★　★

Next morning when Heidi woke up she looked at once for her friend. But Klara wasn't there. Heidi scrambled down the ladder and ran outdoors.

Then she saw what had happened. Her grandfather had already been up to the hayloft and carried the invalid down. He had wrapped her up with all the tenderness of a trained nurse, put her into her wheel-chair and wheeled her out into the sunshine.

Klara was breathing in the spicy air as though it were good enough to eat.

'Oh, if I could only stay up here for ever, Heidi!' she said, and her eyes were full of longing.

[53]

Grandfather joined the two children. He was carrying two bowls of milk. Klara drank hers greedily, and again accepted a second bowl. In Frankfurt, Heidi remembered, Fräulein Rottenmeier could never get Klara to eat anything.

Peter appeared with his herd of goats. Swan and Bear joined, him but this morning Heidi did not. She wanted to stay with Klara. Peter went on up the mountain, grumbling.

The Alm-Uncle had only one thought in his head, to make Klara's cheeks as pink as Heidi's. He longed to see Klara's thin little body plumper and a sparkle come into her pale, tired eyes.

He fed the goats on special herbs so that their milk would be richer. He pushed Klara's wheel-chair as far as he could across the meadows. After she had been there a couple of weeks he said to her every morning:

'Try to stand on the ground for a moment.'

Klara tried, but she couldn't. It hurt her so much that she clung to him for support. But every day he made her try again.

The summer days became lovelier and lovelier. Heidi had never seen the mountain more beautiful. The only thing that upset her was that Klara couldn't come very far from the hut in her wheel-chair. She had to tell Klara about the fields of buttercups higher up the mountain and the rock-roses and bright blue gentians which grew near the cliffs where Peter took the goats. If only Klara could see all this with her own eyes!

There was one way. Grandfather thought of it. It was that he and Peter should push her up in the wheel-chair. It would be a long and difficult climb, and Peter was not very pleased with the idea. But the girls were enthusiastic. If the

He gave it a kick and a violent push

day was warm and fair Heidi and Klara should both go to-
morrow up into the high mountains with a picnic and stay
all day with Peter and watch over the goats.

They were so excited at the thought that they could hardly
go to sleep that night.

* * * * *

Early next morning before the sun was up the Alm-Uncle
came out of the hut to see what sort of day it was going to
be. Over the jagged peak of the Falcon's Nest there was
a pale, golden light. In the deep green valleys the shadows
slowly began to fade. A faint breeze rustled in the fir trees.

The old man sniffed the dawn with approval. He knew

the mountain weather well and it was going to be a perfect day.

He went into the hut and brought out Klara's wheel-chair in which she was to make the journey. Then he began carefully to pack the picnic basket, letting the two children sleep for a few minutes longer.

While he was inside the hut Peter came up with his herd of goats. The first thing Peter saw was the wheel-chair. He stared at it angrily. To Peter the chair seemed like an enemy. To him it meant Klara—and Klara was the reason why he never had Heidi alone to himself these days. Peter suddenly found himself hating that chair.

He looked around. There was no one in sight. Then, scarcely knowing what he did, he rushed at the wheel-chair and gave it a kick and a violent push. He saw it begin to roll away down the slope of the mountain, faster and faster, gaining speed as it went. Peter saw it bounce from boulder to boulder and heard it, in the valley far below, break into a hundred pieces.

He laughed out loud as he saw it smash up. Now, he thought, the stranger from Frankfurt would no longer have any means of moving about, and that meant she would have to go away.

At that moment the Alm-Uncle came out of the hut with Klara in his arms. Heidi beside them ran forward to find the wheel-chair. She was just in time to hear the crash echoing in the valley below.

'The wind must have blown it away,' she wailed.

'Now we can't go,' Klara whimpered.

Both children were heart-broken. They had looked forward so much to to-day's outing.

'We shall certainly go,' the Alm-Uncle said firmly, 'just as we planned.'

He called to Peter who was pretending to be very busy with the goats across the field and told him to come. He and Peter, he said, would have to carry Klara all the way. They made a kind of human chair for Klara with their crossed hands and began the long slow climb. Before it was half over poor Peter was so tired he wished he had never pushed the wheel-chair over the edge of the hill.

At last they came to the high alpine meadow where the goats were to graze that day. The Alm-Uncle spread rugs out on a sunny slope and made Klara comfortable. It was much nicer, she said, than any chair could be. The old man put their picnic basket in the shade of a scrub oak tree and promised to come back to fetch them towards evening. Meanwhile he had to go down the valley and see if the remains of the wheel-chair could be found and repaired.

Above the meadow the sky was cloudless and deep blue. Beyond, on the slopes of the Falcon's Nest, Klara could see the great snowfield, which never melted, gleaming in the sunlight like a million diamonds. Higher still, the jagged mountain peaks stood out proudly against the sky.

Klara had never felt happier. Lying there she felt she could almost reach out and touch all this heavenly beauty. Around her in the meadow the goats peacefully nibbled the rich, green grass.

Klara had begun to know the goats by this time and like Heidi, could call each by its own name. Swan and Bear were, of course, her special favourites. Sometimes they would leave off grazing and come up to her, rubbing their heads against her shoulders to show their friendliness and affection.

The morning passed so pleasantly that it was soon gone. Peter, who had climbed up the hill to have a peaceful nap

[57]

'Now you won't be alone'

by himself, woke up and began to think about the picnic basket. He knew that it would contain a special treat to-day, perhaps even sausages.

Heidi had just remembered that around the cliff there was a wonderful show of rock-roses. She longed to go and see them, but she remembered that her friend couldn't come with her.

'Would you mind very much,' she asked shyly, 'if I left you alone just for a minute? I could bring you some rock-roses. But wait a minute . . .'

She ran to the goats and put her arms around a baby kid whose name was Snowdrop. She brought Snowdrop to Klara. Klara offered it a tuft of grass and the little kid nestled up to her lovingly.

[58]

'Now you won't be alone,' Heidi said as she skipped away.

Klara stroked Snowdrop and gave her more grass to eat. Snowdrop looked into Klara's eyes with such love and trust that Klara's heart grew tender. It was good to feel that the little animal expected something of her—nice to look after a living creature yourself, instead of always being looked after by others. If only she could help others and not always have to be helped herself!

At that moment Klara heard Heidi's excited voice.

'Oh, Klara!' Heidi called, appearing round the cliff. 'Such heavenly rock-roses! You must come and see ... Oh,' she broke off suddenly. She had forgotten that Klara couldn't walk.

Klara smiled sadly. Then Heidi said: 'But Peter and I can carry you. Peter! Come down here at once.'

Peter at first refused to come, but Heidi pointed at the picnic basket and shook her head. Peter understood what she meant. If he didn't obey, he wouldn't get the lion's share of the dinner as he usually did. He came down unwillingly.

'But I'm too big for you,' Klara said.

This was true, for she was a head taller than Heidi and as big as Peter himself. Nevertheless the two of them got her on to her feet. Klara swayed and nearly fell down again.

'Does it hurt so much?' Heidi asked.

Klara was just about to say that it did.

Then she suddenly realised that it didn't!

She took a staggering step forward. It didn't hurt at all! For a moment she didn't understand what had happened. She had walked, without holding on to Peter and Heidi. She had walked alone!

For the first time in her life Klara Sesemann was walking!

* * * * *

When the Alm-Uncle came up for the children that evening he caught their excitement even from a distance. Heidi came rushing towards him, her eyes dancing with joy.

'Klara can do it!' she shouted. 'Klara can walk '

And sure enough, staggering behind her, very uncertain of herself and yet standing upright, came Klara herself. To himself the Alm-Uncle murmured a silent thanks to God.

But he carried the child back to the hut just the same, so that she should not overstrain herself. He decided to run down to Dörfli at once to tell Klara's grandmother what had happened, but the two little girls had a better idea. This was to wait until next week when Lady Sesemann was expected, and then to surprise her.

The old man agreed. For the rest of that week he took Klara for short journeys around the hut, teaching her how to walk as a baby is taught. The exercise made Klara hungrier than ever. She ate so much during those days that she became almost as plump and rosy-cheeked as Heidi herself.

The day came when Klara's grandmother again made the trip up the mountain. The children saw her coming on the horse and they waited, sitting on their stools in front of the door.

Nearer and nearer came the horse. The children didn't move. Grandmama dismounted, looking rather surprised.

'Klara,' she said, 'why aren't you sitting in your wheel-chair?' She looked at her more closely and exclaimed: 'Child! I hardly recognise you. Why, your cheeks are as red as an apple!'

Then Heidi rose from her stool. She gave Klara her arm and Klara rose too. Together the two children started walking calmly away, as if they were going off for a stroll together.

Together the children started walking calmly away

Lady Sesemann could not believe her eyes. She stared at them, and then rushed after them. She caught Klara in her arms, hugging her and kissing her. She laughed and laughed until the tears ran down her cheeks. She could think of absolutely nothing to say. So she kissed Heidi too, and turned to the Alm-Uncle who was enjoying the scene with a quiet smile.

She seized both his hands in hers. 'How can I even begin to thank you!' she cried.

'We must thank the good Lord's sunshine and the mountain air,' he said.

'Yes, and Swan and Bear's good milk,' Klara added.

'Yes,' the old lady said, 'and your good care of her.' She

[61]

added under her breath so that the others didn't hear: 'And Heidi's faith and her prayers . . .'

She sent off a telegram that same day to Paris to her son. On the first possible train Herr Sesemann arrived in Dörfli. He didn't know why he had been sent for. The telegram simply said: 'Come at once.'

He ran most of the way up the steep path towards the Alm-Uncle's hut in his joy at the thought of seeing his little daughter again.

He paused for breath only when he reached the meadow and was looking at the hut where he'd been told the Alm-Uncle lived. He saw two figures standing at the door, waiting for him. One was Heidi.

But who was the tall young girl with the bright, fair hair and rosy cheeks, and the blue eyes which shone like stars?

Tears suddenly blinded him. She looked like Klara's own mother when he had first seen and loved her. Herr Sesemann wondered if he were awake or dreaming.

'Don't you know me, Papa?' Klara laughed. And she ran into his outstretched arms.

To Herr Sesemann it seemed like magic that his little lame daughter could run.

Lady Sesemann, smiling with pleasure at her son's surprise, came out of the hut to welcome him.

Magic she said it was. The homely magic of the good Alm-Uncle's tender care and the happiness Klara had shared with Heidi in this mountain paradise.

What a dinner they all had that day outside the little hut! Even Peter was invited, though the Alm-Uncle had guessed who it was that had pushed the wheel-chair down the mountain. For, as Klara's grandmother said, the wheel-chair

[62]

What a dinner they all had outside the little hut!

was no longer needed! Peter ate more that day than he usually did in a week and afterwards Herr Sesemann gave him a shilling.

'But what can I ever give Heidi?' Herr Sesemann wondered. 'What can I give her to make up for what she has given me —my daughter's health and happiness?'

He asked Heidi what she wanted. She could have, he said, anything in the world which was in his power to give.

Heidi thought about it for a long time. At last she said:

'What I should like best is my bed in Frankfurt. It was so soft and warm, and had thick pillows and a feather quilt. It would be comfortable and warm in winter for Granny, and she gets so terribly cold.'

[63]

So the bed came to Dörfli and now Granny sleeps so well at night that they say she is beginning to regain her strength. Great boxes of food and clothing also come for her regularly from the Sesemanns' house in Frankfurt.

The little village of Dörfli now has a new house. In it lives the doctor who has decided to spend the rest of his life there looking after the poor people of the village. He and the Alm-Uncle are becoming better friends every day. Both of them feel they have a daughter.

And Heidi, who never knew her own father, knows now that she has two fathers. She loves one as much as she loves the other.

WHAT KATY DID

by Susan Coolidge

KATY'S name was Katy Carr. She lived in the town of Burnet, which wasn't a very big town, but was growing fast. The house she lived in stood on the edge of the town. It was a large square house, white, with green blinds, and had a porch in front, over which roses and clematis made a thick bower. Four tall trees shaded the gravel path which led to the front gate. On one side of the house was an orchard; on the other side were wood piles and barns, and an ice-house.

There were six of the Carr children — four girls and two boys. Katy, the oldest, was twelve years old; little Phil, the youngest, was four, and the rest fitted in between.

Dr. Carr, their papa, was a dear, kind, busy man, who was away from home all day, and sometimes all night, too, taking care of sick people. The children hadn't any mamma. She had died when Phil was a baby, four years before my story begins.

In place of their mamma, there was Aunt Izzie, papa's sister, who came to take care of them when mamma went away on that long journey, from which, for so many months, the little ones kept hoping she might return. Aunt Izzie was a small woman, sharp-faced and thin, rather old-looking, and very neat and particular about everything. She meant to be kind to the children, but they puzzled her much, because they were not a bit like herself when she was a child. Aunt Izzie had been a gentle, tidy little thing, who loved to sit as Curly Locks did, sewing long seams in the parlour, and to have her head patted by older people, and be told that she was a good girl; whereas Katy tore her dress every day, hated sewing, and didn't care a button about being called 'good', while Clover and Elsie shied off like restless ponies when anyone tried to pat their heads.

In fact, there was just one half-hour of the day when Aunt Izzie was really satisfied about her charges, and that was the half-hour before breakfast, when she had made a rule that they were all to sit in their little chairs and learn the Bible verse for the day. At this time she looked at them with pleased eyes; they were all so spick-and-span, with such nicely-brushed clothes and such neatly-combed hair. But the moment the bell rang her comfort was over. From that time on, they were what she called 'not fit to be seen'.

'Clover, go upstairs and wash your hands! Dorry, pick your hat off the floor and hang it on the hook! Not that hook — the third hook from the corner!' These were the kind of things Aunt Izzie was saying all day long. The children liked her pretty well, but they didn't exactly love her, I fear. They called her 'Aunt Izzie' always, never 'Aunty'. Boys and girls will know what *that* meant.

I want to show you the little Carrs, and I don't know that I could ever have a better chance than one day when five out of the six were perched on top of the ice-house, like chickens on a roost. This ice-house was one of their favourite places.

They were all to sit in their little chairs and learn the Bible verse for the day

It was only a low roof set over a hole in the ground, and, as it stood in the middle of the side yard, it always seemed to the children that the shortest road to every place was up one of its slopes and down the other.

Clover, next in age to Katy, sat in the middle. She was a fair, sweet dumpling of a girl, with thick pig-tails of light brown hair, and short-sighted blue eyes, which seemed to hold tears, just ready to fall from under the blue. Really, Clover was the jolliest little thing in the world. Everybody loved her, and she loved everybody, especially Katy, whom she looked up to as one of the wisest people in the world.

Pretty little Phil sat next on the roof to Clover, and she held him tight with her arm. Then came Elsie, a thin, brown child

'There's your old post office'

of eight, with beautiful dark eyes, and crisp, short curls cover-
ing the whole of her small head. Poor little Elsie was the 'odd
one' among the Carrs. She didn't seem to belong exactly to
either the older or the younger children. The great desire and
ambition of her heart was to be allowed to go about with Katy
and Clover and Cecy Hall, and to know their secrets, and be
permitted to put notes into the little post-offices they were
forever fixing up in all sorts of hidden places. But they didn't
want Elsie, and used to tell her to 'run away and play with
the children', which hurt her feelings very much. When she
wouldn't run away, I am sorry to say they ran away from her,
which, as their legs were longest, was easy to do. Poor Elsie,
left behind, would cry bitter tears, and, as she was too proud

to play much with Dorry and John, her principal comfort was tracking the older ones about and discovering their mysteries, especially the post-offices, which were her greatest grievance. Her eyes were bright and quick as a bird's. She would peep and peer, and follow and watch, till at last, in some odd, unlikely place, the crotch of a tree, the middle of the asparagus bed, she spied the little paper box, with its load of notes, all ending with: 'Be sure and not let Elsie know.' Then she would seize the box and, marching up to wherever the others were, she would throw it down, saying defiantly: 'There's your old post-office' but feeling all the time just like crying. Poor little Elsie!

Dorry and Joanna sat on the two ends of the ridge-pole. Dorry was six years old; a pale, podgy boy, with rather a solemn face, and smears of molasses on the sleeve of his jacket. Joanna, whom the children called 'John', and 'Johnnie', was a year younger than Dorry; she had big brave eyes, and a wide rosy mouth, which always looked ready to laugh. These two were great friends, though Dorry seemed like a girl who had got into boy's clothes by mistake, and Johnnie like a boy who, in a fit of fun, had borrowed his sister's frock. And now, as they all sat there chattering and giggling, the window above opened, a happy cry was heard, and Katy's head appeared. In her hand she held a heap of stockings, which she waved triumphantly.

'Hurray!' she cried, 'all done, and Aunt Izzie says we may go. Are you tired out waiting? I couldn't help it, the holes were *so* big, and took so long. Hurry up, Clover, and get the things! Cecy and I will be down in a minute.'

The children jumped up gladly, and slid down the roof. Clover fetched a couple of baskets from the wood-shed. Elsie

Dorry and John loaded themselves with two great bunches of green boughs

ran for her kitten. Dorry and John loaded themselves with two great bunches of green boughs. Just as they were ready, the side-door banged, and Katy and Cecy Hall came into the yard.

I must tell you about Cecy. She was a great friend of the children's, and lived in a house next door. The yards of the houses were only separated by a green hedge, with no gate. Cecy spent about two-thirds of her time at Dr. Carr's, and was exactly like one of the family. She was a neat, dapper, pink-and-white girl, modest and prim in manner, with light shiny hair, which always kept smooth, and slim hands, which never looked dirty. How different from my poor Katy! Katy's hair was forever untidy, her gowns were always catching on

[72]

nails and 'tearing themselves' and, in spite of her age and size, she was as heedless and innocent as a child of six. Katy was the *longest* girl that was ever seen. What she did to make herself grow so, nobody could tell; but there she was — up above papa's ear, and half a head taller than poor Aunt Izzie. Whenever she stopped to think about her height she became very awkward, and felt as if she were all legs and elbows, and angles and joints. Happily, her head was so full of other things, of plans and schemes and fancies of all sorts, that she didn't often take time to remember how tall she was.

*   *   *   *   *

The place to which the children were going was a sort of marshy thicket at the bottom of a field near the house. It wasn't a big thicket, but it looked big, because the trees and bushes grew so closely that you could not see just where it ended. Narrow, winding paths ran here and there, made by the cattle as they wandered to and fro. This place the children called 'Paradise', and to them it seemed as wild and endless and full of adventure as any forest of fairy-land.

The way to Paradise was through a wooden fence. Katy and Cecy climbed it with a hop, skip, and jump, while the smaller ones scrambled underneath. Once past the fence they were fairly in the field, and, with one consent, they all began to run till they reached the entrance of the wood. Then they halted with a certain look of hesitation on their faces.

'Which path shall we go in by?' asked Clover, at last.

'Suppose we vote,' said Katy. 'I say by the Pilgrim's Path.'

'So do I!' chimed in Clover, who always agreed with Katy.

Katy and Cecy climbed it with a hop, skip and jump

'The Path of Peace is nice,' suggested Cecy.

'No, no! We want to go by Sassafras Path!' cried John and Dorry.

However, Katy, as usual, had her way. It was agreed that they should first try Pilgrim's Path, and afterward make a thorough exploration of the whole of their little kingdom, and see all that had happened since last they were there. So in they marched, Katy and Cecy heading the procession, and Dorry, with his great trailing bunch of boughs, bringing up the rear.

The Path of Peace got its name because of its darkness and coolness. High bushes almost met over it, and trees kept it shady, even in the middle of the day. A kind of white flower

They stayed a long while picking bunches of these flowers

grew there, which the children called Pollypods, because they didn't know the real name. They stayed a long while picking bunches of these flowers, and then John and Dorry had to grub up an armful of sassafras roots; so that before they had fairly gone through Toadstool Avenue, Rabbit Hollow, and the rest, the sun was just over their heads, and it was noon.

'I'm getting hungry,' said Dorry.

'Oh, no, Dorry, you mustn't be hungry till the bower is ready!' cried the little girls, alarmed, for Dorry was apt to be upset if he was kept waiting for his meals. So they made haste to build the bower. It did not take long, being made of boughs hung over skipping-ropes, which were tied to a poplar-tree.

When it was done they all cuddled in underneath. It was

[75]

a very small bower — just big enough to hold them, and the baskets, and the kitten. I don't think there would have been room for anybody else, not even another kitten. Katy, who sat in the middle, untied and lifted the lid of the largest basket, while all the rest peeped eagerly to see what was inside.

First came a great many ginger cakes. These were carefully laid on the grass to keep till wanted. Buttered biscuits came next — three apiece, with slices of cold lamb laid in between; and last of all were a dozen hard-boiled eggs, and a layer of thick bread-and-butter, sandwiched with corned-beef. Aunt Izzie had put up lunches for Paradise before, you see, and knew pretty well what to expect in the way of appetite.

Oh, how good everything tasted in that bower, with the fresh wind rustling the poplar leaves, sunshine and sweet wood-smells about them, and birds singing overhead! No grown-up dinner party ever had half so much fun. Each mouthful was a pleasure; and when the last crumb had vanished, Katy produced the second basket, and there, oh, delightful surprise! were seven little pies — molasses pies, baked in saucers — each with a brown top and crisp candified edge, which tasted like toffee and lemon-peel, and all sorts of good things mixed up together.

There was general approval. Even demure Cecy was pleased, and Dorry and John kicked their heels on the ground in joy. Seven pairs of hands were held out at once toward the basket; seven sets of teeth went to work without a moment's delay. In an incredibly short time every bit of pie had disappeared, and a blissful stickiness pervaded the party.

'What shall we do now?' asked Clover, while little Phil tipped the baskets upside down, as if to make sure there was nothing left that could possibly be eaten.

[76]

Little Phil tipped the baskets upside down

'Let's play we're grown up,' said Cecy, 'and tell what we mean to do.'

'Well,' said Clover, 'you begin. What do you mean to do?'

'I mean to have a black silk dress, and pink roses in my bonnet, and a long, white muslin shawl,' said Cecy. 'All the young gentlemen will want me to go and ride, but I shan't notice them at all, because you know I shall always be teaching in Sunday-school, and visiting the poor.'

'Pooh!' said Clover, 'I don't think that would be nice at all. *I'm* going to be a beautiful lady — the most beautiful lady in the world! And I'm going to live in a yellow castle, with yellow pillars to the portico, and a square thing on top. There's going to be a spy-glass in the window, to look out of. I shall wear gold dresses and silver dresses every day, and diamond rings, and have white satin aprons to tie on when I'm dusting, or doing anything dirty. In the middle of my back-yard there will be a pond full of Eau de Cologne, and whenever I want any I shall go just out and dip a bottle in.'

'I mean to have just the same,' cried Elsie, whose imagination was fired by this gorgeous vision, 'only my pond will be the biggest. I shall be a great deal beautifuller, too,' she added.

'You can't,' said Katy from overhead. 'Clover is going to be the most beautiful lady in the world.'

'But I'll be *more* beautiful than the most beautiful,' persisted poor Elsie.

'What'll you be, Johnnie?' asked Clover, anxious to change the subject.

But Johnnie had no clear ideas as to her future. She laughed a great deal, and squeezed Dorry's arm very tight, but that was all. Dorry was more decided.

'I mean to have turkey every day,' he declared, 'and batter-puddings; not boiled ones, you know, but little baked ones with brown shiny tops, and a great deal of pudding sauce to eat on them. And I shall be so big then that nobody will say, "Three helpings is quite enough for a little boy".'

'Oh, Dorry, you pig!' cried Katy, while the others screamed with laughter. By and by John and Dorry trotted away on mysterious errands of their own.

'Wasn't Dorry funny with his turkey?' remarked Cecy, and they all laughed again.

'If you won't tell,' said Katy, 'I'll let you see Dorry's journal. He kept it once for almost two weeks, and then gave it up. I found the book, this morning, in the nursery closet.'

Katy produced it from her pocket

All of them promised, and Katy produced it from her pocket. It began thus:

'*March* 12. — Have resolved to keep a jurnal.

'*March* 13. — Had rost befe for diner, and cabage, and potato and appel sawse, and rice puding. I do not like rice puding when it is like ours. Charley Slack's kind is rele good. Mush and sirup for tea.

'*March* 19. — Forgit what did. John and me saved our pie to take to schule.

'*March* 21. — Forgit what did. Gridel cakes for brekfast. Debby didn't fry enuff.

'*March* 24. — This is Sunday. Corn befe for dinnir. Studdied my Bibel leson. Aunt Issy said I was gredy. Have resollved not to think so much about things to ete. Wish I was a beter boy. Nothing pertikeler for tea.

'*March* 25. — Forgit what did.

'*March* 27. — Forgit what did.

'*March* 29. — Played.

'*March* 31. — Forgit what did.

'*April* 1. — Have dissided not to kepe a jurnal enny more.'

It seemed as if only a minute had passed before the long shadows began to fall, and Mary came to say that all of them must come in to get ready for tea. It was dreadful to have to pick up the empty baskets and go home, feeling that the long, delightful Saturday was over, and that there wouldn't be another for a week.

*   *   *   *   *

Mrs. Knight's school, to which Katy and Clover and Cecy went, stood quite at the other end of the town from Dr. Carr's. It was a low, one-storey building, and had a yard behind it, in which the girls played. Unfortunately, next door to it was Miss Miller's school, with a yard behind it also. Only a high board fence separated the two play-grounds.

A constant feud raged between the two schools. The Knight girls, for some unknown reason, considered themselves genteel and the Miller girls vulgar, and took no pains to conceal this opinion. The Miller girls, on the other hand, replied by making faces through the knot-holes in the fence, and over the top of it when they could get there, which wasn't an easy thing to do, as the fence was pretty high. The Knight girls could make faces too, for all their gentility. Their yard had one great advantage over the other — it had a wood shed, with a climbable

[80]

'Here is the bonnet-string'

roof, and upon this the girls used to sit in rows, turning up their noses at the next yard, and irritating the foe by jeering remarks. 'Knights' and 'Millerites', the two schools called each other; and the feud raged so fiercely, that sometimes it was hardly safe for a Knight to meet a Millerite in the street.

One morning, not long after the day in Paradise, Katy was late. She could not find her things. Her algebra, as she expressed it, had 'gone and lost itself', her slate was missing, and the string was off her sun-bonnet. She ran about, searching for these articles and banging doors, till Aunt Izzie was out of patience.

'As for your algebra,' she said, 'if it is that very dirty book with only one cover, and scribbled all over the leaves, you will find it under the kitchen-table. About your slate, I know nothing, but here is the bonnet-string,' taking it out of her pocket.

'Oh, thank you!' said Katy, hastily sticking it on with a pin.

'Katy Carr!' almost screamed Miss Izzie, 'what *are* you about? Pinning on your bonnet-string! Mercy on me, what shiftless thing will you do next? Now stand still, and don't fidget! You shan't stir till I have sewed it on properly.'

It wasn't easy to 'stand still and not fidget', with Aunt Izzie fussing away and lecturing, and now and then, in a moment of forgetfulness, sticking her needle into one's chin. Katy bore it as well as she could, only shifting perpetually from one foot to the other, and now and then uttering a little snort, like an impatient horse. The minute she was released she flew into the kitchen, seized the algebra, and rushed like a whirlwind to the gate, where good little Clover stood patiently waiting, though all ready herself, and terribly afraid she should be late.

'We shall have to run,' gasped Katy, quite out of breath. 'Aunt Izzie kept me. She has been so horrid!'

They did run as fast as they could, but time ran faster, and before they were halfway to school the town clock struck nine, and all hope was over. This vexed Katy very much for, though often late, she was always eager to be early.

'There,' she said, stopping short. 'I shall just tell Aunt Izzie that it was her fault. It is *too* bad.' And she marched into school in a very cross mood.

A day begun in this manner is pretty sure to end badly, as most of us know. All the morning, things seemed to go wrong. Katy forgot answers twice in her grammar lesson, and lost her place in the class. Her hand shook so when she copied her composition, that Mrs. Knight said it must be done all over again. This made Katy crosser than ever; and almost before she thought, she had whispered to Clover, 'How hateful!' And then, when all who had whispered were asked to stand up, her conscience gave such a twinge that she was forced to get up with the rest, and see a black mark put against her name on the list. The tears came into her eyes and, for fear the other girls would notice them, she made a bolt for the yard as soon as the bell rang, and mounted up all alone to the wood-house roof, where she sat with her back to the school, fighting her tears, and trying to get her face in order before the rest should come.

Miss Miller's clock was about four minutes slower than Mrs. Knight's, so the next playground was empty. It was a warm, breezy day, and as Katy sat there, suddenly a gust of wind came, and seizing her sun-bonnet, which was only half tied on, whirled it across the roof. She clutched after it as it flew, but too late. Once, twice, thrice it flapped, and then it disappeared over the edge, and Katy, flying after, saw it lying, a crumpled lilac heap in the very middle of the enemy's yard.

This was horrible! In another minute the Miller girls would be out. Already she seemed to see them dancing war-dances round the unfortunate bonnet, pinning it on a pole, using it as a football, waving it over the fence, and otherwise treating it as Indians treat a captive taken in war. Was it to be endured? Never! Better die first! Katy set her teeth, and sliding rapidly down the roof, reached the fence, and with one bold leap vaulted into Miss Miller's yard.

Out poured the Millerites, big and little. Their wrath and indignation at this daring invasion cannot be described. With a howl of fury they hurled themselves upon Katy, but she was

They hurled themselves upon Katy

quick as they and, holding the rescued bonnet in her hand, was already halfway up the fence.

There are moments when it is a fine thing to be tall. On this occasion Katy's long legs and arms served her an excellent turn. Nothing but a Daddy-long-legs ever climbed so fast or so wildly as she did now. In one second she had gained the top of the fence, and plunged headlong into the midst of a group of Knights.

I cannot tell you what a commotion ensued. The Knights were beside themselves with pride and triumph. Katy was kissed and hugged, and made to tell her story over and over again. Altogether it was a great day for the school, a day to be remembered. As time went on, Katy, what with the excitement of her adventure, and of being praised by the big girls, grew perfectly reckless, and hardly knew what she did.

A good many of the scholars lived too far from school to go home at noon, and were in the habit of bringing their lunches in baskets and staying all day. Katy and Clover were of this number. This noon, after the dinners were eaten, it was proposed that they should play something in the school-room, and Katy's unlucky star put it into her head to invent a new game, which she called the Game of Rivers.

It was played in the following manner: Each girl took the name of a river, and laid out for herself an appointed path through the room, winding among the desks and benches, and making a low, roaring sound, to imitate the noise of water. Cecy was the Platte; Marianne Brookes, a tall girl, the Mississippi; Alice Blair, the Ohio; Clover, the Penobscot; and so on. They were instructed to run into each other once in a while, because, as Katy said, 'rivers do'.

As for Katy herself, she was 'Father Ocean', and growling horribly, raged up and down the platform where Mrs. Knight usually sat. Every now and then, when the others were at the far end of the room, she would suddenly cry out, 'Now for a meeting of the waters!' whereupon all the rivers, bouncing, bounding, scrambling, screaming, would turn and run toward Father Ocean, while he roared louder than all of them put together, and made short rushes up and down, to represent the movement of waves on a beach.

Such a noise as this beautiful game made was never heard in the town of Burnet before or since. People going by stopped and stared, children cried, and an old lady asked why someone didn't run for a policeman.

Mrs. Knight, coming back from dinner, was much amazed

[85]

to see a crowd of people collected in front of her school. Hurrying in, she threw open the door, and there, to her dismay, was the whole room in a frightful state of confusion and uproar: chairs flung down, desks upset, ink streaming on the floor; while in the midst of the ruin the frantic rivers raced and screamed, and Old Father Ocean, with a face as red as fire, capered like a lunatic on the platform.

'What *does* this mean?' gasped poor Mrs. Knight, almost unable to speak for horror.

All of a sudden, each girl seemed to realize what a condition the room was in, and what a horrible thing she had done.

Katy's heart gave a great thump, but she spoke up bravely: 'I made up the game, and I was Father Ocean,' she said to the astonished Mrs. Knight, who glared at her for a minute, and then replied solemnly: 'Very well, Katy — sit down;' which Katy did, feeling more ashamed than ever.

The afternoon was long and hard. Mrs. Knight did not smile once. The lessons dragged and Katy, after the heat and excitement of the forenoon, began to feel miserable. She had received more than one hard blow during the meetings of the waters, and had bruised herself almost without knowing it, against the desks and chairs. All these places now began to ache. Her head throbbed so that she could hardly see and a lump of something heavy seemed to be lying on her heart.

For a wonder, Dr. Carr was at home that evening. It was always a great treat to the children when this happened, and Katy thought herself happy when, after the little ones had gone to bed, she got papa to herself and told him the whole story.

'Papa,' she said, sitting on his knee, which, big girl as she was, she liked very much to do, 'what is the reason that makes some days so lucky and other days so unlucky? Now, to-day began all wrong, and everything that happened in it was wrong; and on other days I begin right, and all goes right, straight through. If Aunt Izzie hadn't kept me in the morning, I shouldn't have lost my mark, and then I shouldn't have been cross, and then *perhaps* I shouldn't have got in my other scrapes.'

'But what made Aunt Izzie keep you, Katy?'

'To sew on the string of my bonnet, Papa.'

'But how did it happen that the string was off?'

'Well,' said Katy, reluctantly, 'I am afraid that was *my* fault, for it came off on Tuesday, and I didn't fasten it on.'

'So you see, we must go back before Aunt Izzie for the beginning of this unlucky day of yours, Childie. Did you ever hear the old saying about "For the want of a nail the shoe was lost"?'

'No, never — tell it to me ' cried Katy, who still loved stories as well as when she was three years old.

So Dr. Carr repeated:

'For the want of a nail the shoe was lost,
For the want of a shoe the horse was lost,
For the want of a horse the rider was lost,
For the want of the rider the battle was lost,
For the want of the battle the kingdom was lost,
And all for want of a horse-shoe nail.'

'Oh, Papa!' exclaimed Katy, giving him a great hug as she got off his knee, 'I see what you mean! Who would have thought such a little speck of a thing as not sewing on my string could make a difference? But I don't believe I shall get into any more scrapes, for I shan't ever forget:

"For the want of a nail the shoe was lost".'

'I'm going out to drink tea with Mrs. Hall,' Aunt Izzie told Katy

But I am sorry to say that my poor thoughtless Katy *did* forget, and did get into another scrape, and that no later than the very next Monday.

'I'm going out to drink tea with Mrs. Hall and attend the evening lecture,' Aunt Izzie told Katy. 'Be sure that Clover gets her lesson, and if Cecy comes over as usual, you must send her home early. All of you must be in bed by nine.'

'Yes'm,' said Katy; but I fear she was not attending much, but thinking, in her secret soul, how jolly it was to have Aunt Izzie go out for once.

Miss Carr was very faithful to her duties, she seldom left the children, so whenever she did, they felt a certain sense of novelty and freedom, which was dangerous as well as pleasant.

Still, I am sure that on this occasion Katy meant no mischief. Like all excitable people, she seldom did *mean* to do wrong, she just did whatever came into her head. Supper passed off successfully, and all might have gone well had it not been that after the lessons were learned and Cecy had come in, they fell to talking about 'Kikeri'.

Kikeri was a game which had been very popular with them a year before. They had invented it themselves, and chosen for it this queer name out of on old fairy story. It was a sort of mixture of Blind-man's-buff and Tag — only instead of anyone's eyes being bandaged, they all played in the dark. One of the children would stay out in the hall, which was dimly lighted from the stairs, while the others hid themselves in the nursery. When they were all hidden, they would call out 'Kikeri' as a signal for the one in the hall to come in and find them. Of course, coming from the light they could see nothing, while the others could see only dimly. It was very exciting to stand crouching up in a corner and watch the dark figure stumbling about and feeling to right and left, while every now and then somebody, just escaping his clutches, would slip past and gain the hall, which was 'Freedom Castle', with a joyful shout of 'Kikeri, Kikeri, Kikeri, Ki!' Whoever was caught had to take the place of the catcher. For a long time this game was the delight of the Carr children; but so many scratches and black-and-blue spots came of it, and so many of the nursery things were knocked down and broken, that at last Aunt Izzie issued an order that it should not be played any more. This was almost a year ago, but talking of it now put it into their heads to want to try it again.

It was certainly splendid fun. Once Clover climbed up on the mantelpiece and sat there, and when Katy, who was finder,

Once Clover climbed up on the mantelpiece and sat there

groped about a little more wildly than usual, she caught hold of Clover's foot and couldn't imagine where it came from. Dorry got a hard knock, and cried, and at another time Katy's dress caught on the bureau-handle and was frightfully torn, but these were too much affairs of every day to interfere in the least with the pleasures of Kikeri. In the excitement, time went on much faster than any of them dreamed. Suddenly, in the midst of the noise, came a sound — the sharp distinct slam of the carriage-door. Aunt Izzie had returned!

The dismay and confusion of that moment! Cecy slipped downstairs like an eel, and fled on the wings of fear along the path which led to her home. Mrs. Hall, as she bade Aunt Izzie good night and shut Dr. Carr's front door behind her with

Cecy slipped downstairs like an eel

a bang, might have been struck with the singular fact that
a distant bang came from her own front door like a sort of echo.
But she was not a suspicious woman; and when she went
upstairs there were Cecy's clothes neatly folded on a chair, and
Cecy herself in bed, fast asleep, only with a little more colour
than usual in her cheeks.

Meantime, Aunt Izzie was on *her* way upstairs, and such
a panic prevailed in the nursery! Katy left it, and basely
scuttled off to her own room, where she went to bed with all
possible speed. But the others found it much harder to go to bed.
There were so many of them, all getting into each other's way,
and with no lamp to see by. Dorry and John popped under the
clothes half-undressed, Elsie disappeared, and Clover, too late

for either, fell on her knees, with her face buried in a chair, and began to say her prayers very hard indeed.

Aunt Izzie, coming in with a candle in her hand, stood in the doorway, astonished at the sight. She sat down and waited for Clover to get through, while Clover, on her part, didn't dare to get through, but went on repeating 'Now I lay me' over and over again, in a sort of despair. At last Aunt Izzie said very grimly: 'That will do, Clover, you can get up!' and Clover rose, feeling like a culprit, which she was.

Aunt Izzie at once began to undress her, and while doing so asked so many questions that before long she had got at the truth of the whole matter. She gave Clover a sharp scolding, and leaving her to wash her tearful face, she went to the bed where John and Dorry lay, fast asleep, and snoring as loudly as they knew how. Something strange in the appearance of the bed made her look more closely. She lifted the clothes, and there, sure enough, they were — half dressed, and with their school-boots on.

Such a shake as Aunt Izzie gave the little scamps at this discovery would have roused a couple of dormice. Much against their will, John and Dorry were forced to wake up, and be slapped and scolded, and made ready for bed, Aunt Izzie standing over them all the while, like a dragon. She had just tucked them in, when for the first time she missed Elsie.

'Where is my poor little Elsie?' she exclaimed.

'In bed,' said Clover meekly.

'In bed!' repeated Aunt Izzie, much amazed. Then, stooping down, she gave a vigorous pull. The trundle-bed came into view, and sure enough, there was Elsie, in full dress, shoes and all, but so fast asleep that not all Aunt Izzie's shakes, and pinches, and calls, were able to rouse her. Her clothes were

Aunt Izzie, coming in with a candle in her hand, stood in the doorway

taken off, her boots unlaced, her nightgown put on; but through it all Elsie slept, and she was the only one of the children who did not get the scolding she deserved that dreadful night.

Katy did not even pretend to be asleep when Aunt Izzie went to her room. Her tardy conscience had waked up, and she was lying in bed, very miserable at having drawn the others into a scrape as well as herself, and at the failure of her last set of resolutions about 'setting an example to the younger ones'. So unhappy was she that Aunt Izzie's severe words were almost a relief, and though she cried herself to sleep, it was rather from the burden of her own thoughts than because she had been scolded.

They never played Kikeri again from that day to this.

One day in July, Katy and Clover come running home from school.

They burst open the front door and raced upstairs crying 'Hurrah! hurrah! vacation's begun. Aunt Izzie, vacation's begun!' Then they stopped short, for lo! the upper hall was all in confusion. Sounds of beating and dusting came from the spare room. Tables and chairs were standing about; and a cot-bed, which seemed to be taking a walk all by itself, had stopped short at the head of the stairs, and barred the way.

'Why, how queer!' said Katy, trying to get past. 'What *can* be going to happen? Oh, there's Aunt Izzie! Aunt Izzie, who's coming? What *are* you moving the things out of the Blue-room for?'

'Oh, gracious! is that you?' replied Aunt Izzie, who looked very hot and flurried. 'Now, children, it's no use for you to stand there asking questions; I haven't got time to answer them. Go right downstairs, both of you, and don't come up this way again till after tea. I've just as much as I can possibly attend to till then.'

'Just tell us what's going to happen, and we will,' cried the children.

'Your Cousin Helen is coming to visit us,' said Miss Izzie, curtly, and disappeared into the Blue-room.

This was news indeed. Katy and Clover ran downstairs in great excitement, and after consulting a little, retired to the loft to talk it over in peace and quiet. Cousin Helen coming! It seemed as strange as if Queen Victoria, gold crown and all, had invited herself to tea. Or as if some character out of a book, Robinson Crusoe, say, had driven up with a trunk, and announced his intention of spending a week. For to the imaginations of the children, Cousin Helen was as interesting and

The upper hall was all in confusion

unreal as anybody in the Fairy Tales — Cinderella, or Blue-beard, or dear Red Riding-Hood herself.

None of them had ever seen her. Philly said he was sure she hadn't any legs, because she never went away from home, and lay on a sofa all the time. But the rest knew that this was because Cousin Helen was ill. Papa always went to visit her twice a year, and he liked to talk to the children about her, and tell how sweet and patient she was, and what a pretty room she lived in. Katy and Clover had 'played Cousin Helen' so long that now they were frightened as well as glad at the idea of seeing the real one.

'What do you suppose she looks like?' went on Clover.

'Something like "Lucy", in Mrs. Sherwood, I suppose, with

blue eyes, and curls, and a long, straight nose. And she'll keep her hands clasped *so* all the time, and wear "frilled wrappers", and lie on the sofa perfectly still, and never smile, but just look patient. We'll have to take off our boots in the hall, Clover, and go upstairs in stockinged feet, so as not to make a noise.'

'Won't it be funny!' giggled Clover.

The time seemed very long till the next afternoon, when Cousin Helen was expected.

Five o'clock came at last. They all sat on the steps waiting for the carriage. At last it drove up. Papa was on the box. He motioned the children to stand back. Then he very carefully lifted Cousin Helen in his arms and brought her in.

'Oh, there are the chicks!' were the first words the children heard, in *such* a gay, pleasant voice. 'Do set me down somewhere, Uncle, I want to see them so much!'

So papa put Cousin Helen on the hall sofa. Aunt Izzie fetched a pillow, and when she was made comfortable, Dr. Carr called to the little ones.

'Cousin Helen wants to see you,' he said.

'Indeed I do,' said the bright voice. 'So this is Katy? Why, what a splendid tall girl Katy is! And this is Clover,' kissing her; 'and *this* dear little Elsie. You all look as natural as possible — just as if I had seen you before.' And she hugged them all round, not as if it was polite to like them because they were relations, but as if she had loved them and wanted them all her life.

There was something in Cousin Helen's face and manner which made the children at home with her at once. Even Philly, who had backed away with his hands behind him, after staring hard for a minute or two, came up with a sort of rush to get his share of kissing.

'So this is Katy?'

Still, Katy's first feeling was one of disappointment. Cousin Helen was not at all like 'Lucy', in Mrs. Sherwood's story. Her nose turned up the least bit in the world. She had brown hair, which didn't curl, a brown skin, and bright eyes which danced when she laughed or spoke. Her face was thin but except for that you wouldn't have guessed that she was sick. She didn't fold her hands, and she didn't look patient, but full of life and merry. Her dress wasn't a 'frilled wrapper', but a sort of loose travelling thing of pretty grey stuff, with a rose-coloured bow, and bracelets.

All the dreams Katy had had about the 'saintly invalid' seemed to take wings and fly away. But the more she watched Cousin Helen the more she seemed to like her, and to feel as if she were nicer than the imaginary person which she and Clover had invented.

'She looks just like other people, doesn't she?' whispered Cecy, who had come over to have a peep at the new arrival.

'Y-e-s,' replied Katy, doubtfully, 'only a great, great deal prettier.'

Next morning the children got up very early. They were so glad that it was vacation. If it hadn't been, they would have been forced to go to school without seeing Cousin Helen, for she didn't wake till late. They grew so impatient of the delay, and went upstairs so often to listen at the door, and see if she were moving, that Aunt Izzie finally had to order them off. Katy rebelled against this order a good deal, but she consoled herself by going into the garden and picking the prettiest flowers she could find to give to Cousin Helen the moment she should see her.

When Aunt Izzie let her go up, Cousin Helen was lying on the sofa all dressed for the day in a fresh blue muslin, with blue ribbons, and pretty bronze slippers with rosettes on the toes. The sofa had been wheeled round with its back to the light. There was a cushion with a pretty fluted cover, that Katy had never seen before, and several other things were scattered about, which gave the room quite a different air. All the house was neat, but somehow Aunt Izzie's rooms never were *pretty*. Children's eyes are quick to see such things, and Katy saw at once that the Blue-room had never looked like this.

Cousin Helen was white and tired, but her eyes and smile were as bright as ever. She was delighted with the flowers, which Katy presented rather shyly.

'Oh, how lovely!' she said; 'I must put them in water immediately. Katy, dear, won't you bring that little vase on the

Picking the prettiest flowers she could find

bureau and set it on this chair beside me? And please pour a little water into it first.'

'What a beauty!' cried Katy, as she lifted the graceful white cup on its gilt stand. 'Is it yours, Cousin Helen?'

'Yes, it is my pet vase. It stands on a little table beside me at home, and I knew I'd miss it if I didn't bring it along.'

Then she began to arrange the flowers, touching each separate one gently, and as if she loved it.

'What a queer noise!' she exclaimed, suddenly stopping.

It *was* queer — a sort of snuffling and snorting sound, as if a walrus was moving up and down in the hall. Katy opened the door. Behold! there were John and Dorry, very red in the face from flattening their noses against the keyhole, in a vain attempt to see if Cousin Helen were up and ready to receive company.

'Oh, let them come in!' cried Cousin Helen from her sofa.

So they came in, followed, before long, by Clover and Elsie. Such a merry morning did they have! Cousin Helen seemed to have a perfect genius for story-telling, and for suggesting games which could be played about her sofa, and did not make more noise than she could bear. Aunt Izzie, dropping in about eleven o'clock, found them having such a good time that almost before she knew it, *she* was drawn into the game too. Nobody had ever heard of such a thing before! There sat Aunt Izzie on the floor, with three long lamp-lighters stuck in her hair, playing, 'I'm a genteel lady, always genteel', in the jolliest manner possible. The children were so enchanted at the sight that they could hardly attend to the game, and were always forgetting how many 'horns' they had. Clover thought that really Cousin Helen must be a witch and papa, when he came home at noon, said almost the same thing.

'What *have* you been doing to them, Helen?' he asked, as he opened the door and saw the merry circle on the carpet. Aunt Izzie's hair was half pulled down, and Philly was rolling over and over in fits of laughter. But Cousin Helen said she hadn't done anything, and pretty soon papa was on the floor too, playing away as fast as the rest.

'I must put a stop to this,' he cried, when everybody was tired of laughing, and everybody's head was stuck as full of paper quills as a porcupine's back. 'Cousin Helen will be worn out. Run away, all of you, and don't come near this door again till the clock strikes four. Do you hear, chicks? Run — run! Shoo! shoo!'

The children scuttled away like a brood of fowls — all but

Behold! there were John and Dorry

Katy. 'Oh, Papa, I'll be *so* quiet!' she pleaded. 'Mightn't I stay just till the dinner-bell rings?'

'Do let her!' said Cousin Helen. So papa said, 'Yes.'

It was no use, after this, for Aunt Izzie to make rules about going into the Blue-room. She might as well have ordered flies to keep away from a sugar-bowl. By hook or by crook, the children *would* get upstairs. Whenever Aunt Izzie went in, she was sure to find them there, just as close to Cousin Helen as they could get. Helen begged her not to interfere.

'We have only three or four days to be together,' she said. 'Let them come as much as they like. It won't hurt me a bit.'

Little Elsie clung with a passionate love to this new friend. Cousin Helen had sharp eyes. She saw the wistful look in

Elsie's face at once, and took special pains to be sweet and tender to her. This made Katy jealous. She couldn't bear to share her cousin with anybody.

When the last evening came, and they went up after tea to the Blue-room, Cousin Helen was opening a box which had just come by Express.

'It is a Good-bye Box,' she said. 'All of you must sit down in a row, and when I hide my hands behind me, *so*, you must choose in turn which you will take.'

So they all chose in turn, 'Which hand will you have, the right or the left?' and Cousin Helen, with the air of a wise fairy, brought out from behind her pillow something pretty for each one. First came a vase exactly like her own, which Katy had admired so much. Katy screamed with delight as it was placed in her hands:

'Oh, how lovely! how lovely!' she cried. 'I'll keep it as long as I live and breathe.'

'If you do, it'll be the first time you ever kept anything for a week without breaking it,' remarked Aunt Izzie.

Next came a pretty purple purse for Clover. It was just what she wanted, for she had lost hers. Then a sweet little locket on a bit of velvet ribbon, which Cousin Helen tied round Elsie's neck.

'There's a piece of my hair in it,' she said. 'Why, Elsie, darling, what's the matter? Don't cry so!'

'Oh, you're s-o beautiful and s-o sweet!' sobbed Elsie; 'and you're go-o-ing away.'

Dorry had a box of dominoes, and John a solitaire board. For Phil there appeared an attractive book — *The History of the Robber Cat*.

Next day came the sad parting. All the little ones stood at

the gate, to wave their pocket-handkerchiefs as the carriage drove away. When it was quite out of sight, Katy rushed off to 'weep a little weep', all by herself.

'Papa said he wished we were all like Cousin Helen,' she thought, as she wiped her eyes, 'and I mean to try, though I don't suppose if I tried a thousand years I should ever get to be half so good. I'll study, and keep my things in order, and be ever so kind to the little ones. Dear me — if only Aunt Izzie was Cousin Helen, how easy it would be! Never mind — I'll think about her all the time, and I'll begin tomorrow.'

★ ★ ★ ★ ★

'Tomorrow I will begin,' thought Katy, as she dropped asleep that night. How often we all do so! And what a pity it is that when morning comes and tomorrow is today, we so often wake up feeling quite differently, careless or impatient, and not a bit inclined to do the fine things we planned overnight.

You know how, if we begin the day in a cross mood, all sorts of unfortunate accidents seem to occur to add to our vexations. The very first thing Katy did this morning was to break her precious vase — the one Cousin Helen had given her.

It was standing on the bureau with a little cluster of blush-roses in it. The bureau had a swing-glass. While Katy was brushing her hair, the glass tipped a little so that she could not see. At a good-humoured moment, this accident wouldn't have troubled her much. But being out of temper to begin with, it made her angry. She gave the glass a violent push. The lower part swung forward, there was a smash, and the first thing Katy knew the blush-roses lay scattered all over the floor, and Cousin Helen's pretty present was ruined.

[103]

The blush-roses lay scattered all over the floor

Katy just sat down on the carpet and cried as hard as if she had been Phil himself. Aunt Izzie heard her, and came in.

'I'm very sorry,' she said, picking up the broken glass, 'but it's no more than I expected, you're so careless, Katy. Now don't sit there in that foolish way! Get up and dress yourself. You'll be late for breakfast.'

'What's the matter?' asked papa, noticing Katy's red eyes as she took her seat at the table.

'I've broken my vase,' said Katy, dolefully.

'It was extremely careless of you to put it in such a dangerous place,' said her aunt. 'You might have known that the glass would swing and knock it off.' Then, seeing a big tear fall in the middle of Katy's plate, she added: 'Really, Katy, you're too big to behave like a baby. Why, Dorry would be ashamed to do so. Please control yourself!'

This snub did not improve Katy's temper. She went on with her breakfast in sulky silence.

'What are you all going to do today?' asked Dr. Carr, hoping to give things a more cheerful turn.

'Swing!' cried John and Dorry both together. 'Alexander's put us up a splendid one in the woodshed.'

'No, you're not,' said Aunt Izzie, in a firm voice; 'the swing is not to be used till tomorrow. Remember that, children. Not till tomorrow. And not then, unless I give you leave.'

This was unwise of Aunt Izzie. She would have done better to have explained further. The truth was that Alexander, in putting up the swing, had cracked one of the staples which fastened it to the roof. He meant to get a new one in the course of the day, and, meantime, he had warned Miss Carr to let no one use the swing, because it really was not safe. If she had told this to the children, all would have been right, but Aunt Izzie's theory was that young people must obey their elders without explanation. Katy went out by the side-door into the yard soon after this. As she passed the shed, the new swing caught her eye.

'How exactly like Aunt Izzie,' she thought, 'ordering the children not to swing till she gives them leave! I suppose she thinks it's too hot. *I* shan't mind her, anyhow.'

She seated herself in the swing. It was a first-rate one, with a broad comfortable seat, and thick new ropes. The place felt cool and dark, and the motion of the swing seemed to set the breeze blowing. It waved Katy's hair like a great fan, and made her dreamy and quiet. All sorts of sleepy ideas began to flit through her brain. Swinging to and fro, she gradually rose

The motion of the swing seemed to set the breeze blowing

higher and higher, driving herself along by the motion of her body, and striking the floor smartly with her foot at every sweep. Now she was at the top of the high arched door. Then she could almost touch the cross-beam above it, and through the small square window could see pigeons sitting and pluming themselves on the eaves of the barn, and white clouds blowing over the blue sky.

She had never swung so high before. It was like flying, she thought, and she bent and curved more strongly in the seat, trying to send herself yet higher, and graze the roof with her toes.

Suddenly, at the very highest point of the sweep, there was a sharp noise of cracking. The swing gave a violent twist,

[106]

spun half round, and tossed Katy into the air. She clutched the rope — felt it dragged from her grasp — then, down — down — down — she fell. All grew dark, and she knew no more.

When she opened her eyes she was lying on the sofa in the dining-room. Clover was kneeling beside her with a pale, scared face, and Aunt Izzie was dropping something cold and wet on her forehead.

'What's the matter?' asked Katy, faintly.

'Oh, she's alive — she's alive!' and Clover put her arms round Katy's neck and sobbed.

'Hush, dear!' Aunt Izzie's voice sounded unusually gentle. 'You've had a bad tumble, Katy. Don't you remember?'

'A tumble? Oh, yes — out of the swing!' said Katy, as it all came slowly back to her. 'Did the rope break, Aunt Izzie? I can't remember about it.'

'No, Katy, the rope didn't break. The staple drew out of the roof. It was a cracked one, and not safe. Why, don't you recollect my telling you not to swing today? Did you forget?'

'No, Aunt Izzie — I didn't forget. I —' But here Katy broke down. She closed her eyes, and big tears rolled from under the lids.

'Don't cry,' whispered Clover, crying herself, 'please don't. Aunt Izzie isn't going to scold you.' But Katy was too weak and shaken not to cry.

'I think I'd like to go upstairs and lie on the bed,' she said. But when she tried to get off the sofa, everything swam before her, and she fell back again on the pillow.

'Why, I can't stand up!' she gasped, looking very much frightened.

'I'm afraid you've given yourself a sprain somewhere,' said

Aunt Izzie was dropping something cold and wet on her forehead

Aunt Izzie, who looked rather frightened herself. 'You'd better lie still a while, dear, before you try to move. Ah, here's the doctor! Well, I *am* glad.' And she went forward to meet him. It wasn't papa, but Dr. Alsop, who lived quite near them.

Dr. Alsop sat down beside the sofa and felt Katy's pulse. Then he began feeling all over her.

'Can you move this leg?' he asked.

Katy gave a feeble kick.

'And this?'

The kick was a good deal more feeble.

'Did that hurt you?' asked Dr. Alsop, seeing a look of pain on her face.

'Yes, a little,' replied Katy, trying hard not to cry.

'In your back, eh? Was the pain high up or low down?'
And the doctor punched Katy's spine for some minutes, making her squirm uneasily.

'I'm afraid she's done some mischief,' he said at last, 'but it's impossible to tell yet exactly what. It may be only a twist, or a slight sprain,' he added, seeing a look of terror on Katy's face. 'You'd better get her upstairs and undress her as soon as you can, Miss Carr. I'll leave a prescription to rub her with.' And Dr. Alsop took out a bit of paper and began to write.

'Oh, must I go to bed?' said Katy. 'How long will I have to stay there, doctor?'

'That depends on how fast you get well,' replied the doctor; 'not long, I hope. Perhaps only a few days.'

'A few days!' repeated Katy, in a despairing tone.

After the doctor was gone, Aunt Izzie and Debby lifted Katy, and carried her slowly upstairs. It was not easy, for every motion hurt her, and the sense of being helpless hurt most of all. She couldn't help crying after she was undressed and put into bed. It all seemed so dreadful and strange. If only papa was here, she thought. But Dr. Carr had gone into the country to see somebody who was very sick, and couldn't possibly be back till tomorrow.

Such a long, long afternoon that was! Aunt Izzie sent up some dinner, but Katy couldn't eat. Her lips were parched and her head ached violently. The sun began to pour in, the room grew warm. Flies buzzed in the window, and tormented her by lighting on her face. Little prickles of pain ran up and down her back. She lay with her eyes shut, because it hurt to keep them open, and all sorts of uneasy thoughts went rushing through her mind.

'Perhaps, if my back is really sprained, I shall have to lie

[109]

here as much as a week,' she said to herself. 'Oh, dear, dear! I *can't*. The vacation is only eight weeks and I was going to do such lovely things! How can people be so patient as Cousin Helen when they have to lie still? Won't she be sorry when she hears! Was it really yesterday that she went away? It seems a year. If only I hadn't got into that nasty old swing!' As these thoughts ran through her mind, her head grew hotter and her position in the bed more uncomfortable.

Aunt Izzie slept in her room that night. Katy was feverish. When morning came, and Dr. Carr returned, he found her in a good deal of pain, hot and restless, with wide open, anxious eyes.

'Papa!' she cried the first thing, 'must I lie here as much as a week?'

'My darling, I'm afraid you must,' replied her father, who looked worried, and very grave.

'Dear, dear!' sobbed Katy, 'how can I bear it?'

★ ★ ★ ★ ★

If anybody had told Katy, that first afternoon, that at the end of a week she would still be in bed, and in pain, and with no time fixed for getting up, I think it would have almost killed her. She was so restless and eager that to lie still seemed one of the hardest things in the world.

Yet there came a time when Katy didn't ever ask to be allowed to get up. A time when sharp, dreadful pain, such as she never imagined before, took hold of her. When days and nights got all confused and tangled up together, and Aunt Izzie never seemed to go to bed. A time when papa was constantly in her room. When other doctors came and stood over

[110]

her, and punched and felt her back, and talked to each other in low whispers. It was all like a long, bad dream, from which she couldn't wake up, though she tried ever so hard.

We will hurry over this time, for it is hard to think of our bright Katy in such a sad plight. By and by the pain grew less, and the sleep quieter. Then, as the pain became easier still, Katy woke up as it were — began to take notice of what was going on about her; to ask questions.

'How long have I been ill?' she asked one morning.

'It is four weeks yesterday,' replied papa.

'Four weeks!' said Katy. 'Why, I didn't know it was as long as that. Was I very ill, Papa?'

'Very, dear. But you are a great deal better now.'

'Is the fever well now, Papa? Can I get up again and go downstairs yet?'

'Not yet, I'm afraid,' said Dr. Carr, trying to speak cheerfully.

Katy didn't ask any more questions then. Another week passed, and another. The pain was almost gone. It only came back now and then for a few minutes. She could sleep now, and eat, and be raised in bed without feeling giddy. But still the once active limbs hung heavy and lifeless, and she was not able to walk, or even stand alone.

'My legs feel so queer,' she said one morning; 'they are just like the Prince's legs which were turned to black marble in the *Arabian Nights*. What do you think is the reason, Papa? Won't they feel natural soon?'

'Not soon,' answered Dr. Carr. Then he said to himself, 'Poor child! she had better know the truth.' So he went on aloud, 'I am afraid, my darling, that you must make up your mind to stay in bed a long time.'

[111]

Clover and Cecy would come to sit with her

'How long?' asked Katy, looking frightened; 'a month more?'

'I can't tell exactly how long,' answered her father. 'It may be that you will have to lie here for months, or it may be more. The only cure for such a hurt is time and patience. It is hard, darling' — for Katy began to sob wildly — 'but you have hope to help you along. Think of poor Cousin Helen, bearing all these years without hope!'

'Oh, Papa!' gasped Katy between her sobs, 'doesn't it seem dreadful, that just getting into the swing for a few minutes should do so much harm? Such a little thing as that!'

'Yes, such a little thing!' repeated Dr. Carr, sadly. 'And it was only a little thing, too, forgetting Aunt Izzie's order about the swing. Just for the want of the small "horse-shoe nail" of Obedience, Katy.'

Years afterwards, Katy told somebody that the six longest weeks of her life were those which followed this talk with papa. Now that she knew there was no chance of getting well at once, the days dragged dreadfully. Each seemed duller and dismaller than the day before. She lost heart about herself, and took no interest in anything. Aunt Izzie brought her books, but she didn't want to read, or to sew. Nothing amused her. Clover and Cecy would come to sit with her, but hearing them tell about their games, and the things they had been doing, made her cry so miserably that Aunt Izzie wouldn't let them come often. They were very sorry for Katy, but the room was so gloomy, and Katy so cross, that they didn't mind much not being allowed to see her. In those days Katy made Aunt Izzie keep the blinds shut tight, and she lay in the dark thinking how miserable she was, and how wretched all the rest of her life was going to be.

The first thing which broke in upon this sad state of affairs was a letter from Cousin Helen, which papa brought one morning and handed to Aunt Izzie.

'Helen tells me she is going home this week,' said Aunt Izzie, from the window, where she had gone to read the letter. 'She intends dropping in here for an hour on her way.'

For the next week Katy was feverish with expectation. At last Cousin Helen came. This time Katy was not on the steps to welcome her, but after a little while papa brought Cousin Helen in his arms, and sat her in a big chair beside the bed.

'How dark it is!' she said, after they had kissed each other and talked for a minute or two; 'I can't see your face at all. Would it hurt your eyes to have a little more light?'

'Push the blinds open a little bit, then, Clover'

'Oh, no!' answered Katy. 'It doesn't hurt my eyes, only
I hate to have the sun come in. It makes me feel worse, somehow.'

'Push the blinds open a little bit, then, Clover,' and Clover
did so.

'Now I can see,' said Cousin Helen.

It was a forlorn-looking child enough which she saw lying
before her. Katy's face had grown thin, and her eyes had red
circles about them from continual crying. Her hair had been
brushed twice that morning by Aunt Izzie, but Katy had run
her fingers impatiently through it, till it stood out above her
head like a frowsy bush. Near her was a calico dressing-gown,
which, though clean, was particularly ugly in pattern; and the

[114]

room, for all its tidiness, had a dismal look, with the chairs set up against the wall, and a row of medicine-bottles on the chimney-piece.

'Isn't it horrid?' sighed Katy, as Cousin Helen looked around. 'Everything's horrid. But I don't mind so much now that you've come. Oh, Cousin Helen, I've had such a dreadful, *dreadful* time!'

'I know,' said her cousin, pityingly. 'I've heard all about it, Katy, and I'm so very sorry for you. It is a hard trial, my poor darling.'

'But how do *you* do it?' cried Katy. 'How do you manage to be so sweet and beautiful and patient, when you're feeling badly all the time, and can't do anything, or walk, or stand?' — her voice was lost in sobs.

Cousin Helen didn't say anything for a little while. She just sat and stroked Katy's hand. 'Shall I tell you, Katy, what it seems to me that I should say to myself if I were in your place?'

'Yes, please,' replied Katy, wonderingly.

'Every morning, the first thing when I woke up, I would say to myself: "I am going to get well, so papa thinks. Perhaps it may be tomorrow. So, in case this *should* be the last day of my sickness, let me spend it *beautifully*, and make my sick-room so pleasant that everybody will like to remember it." You can make your room such a delightful place that they will want to come to you! Don't you see, a sick person has one splendid chance — she is always on hand. Everybody who wants her knows just where to go. If people love her, she gets naturally to be the heart of the house.

'Once make the little ones feel that your room is the place of all others to come to when they are tired, or happy, or

[115]

'You can't think how much better I feel'

grieved, or sorry about anything, and that the Katy who lives
there is sure to give them a loving welcome — and the battle
is won. When one's own life is laid aside for a while, as yours
is now, that is the very time to take up other people's lives,
as we can't do when we are scurrying and bustling over our
own affairs. But I didn't mean to preach a sermon. I'm afraid
you're tired.'

'No, I'm not a bit,' said Katy, holding Cousin Helen's hand
tight in hers; 'you can't think how much better I feel. Oh,
Cousin Helen, I *will* try!'

*   *   *   *   *

'What are the children all doing today?' said Katy, 'I haven't seen them since breakfast.'

Aunt Izzie, who was sewing on the other side of the room, looked up from her work.

'I don't know,' she said; 'they're over at Cecy's, or somewhere. They'll be back before long, I guess.'

Her voice sounded a little odd and mysterious, but Katy didn't notice it.

'I thought of such a nice plan yesterday,' she went on. 'That all of them should hang their stockings up here tomorrow night instead of in the nursery. Then I could see them open their presents, you know. Mayn't they, Aunt Izzie? It would be great fun.'

'I don't think there will be any objection,' replied her aunt. She looked as if she were trying not to laugh. Katy wondered what *was* the matter with her.

It was more than two months now since Cousin Helen went away, and winter had fairly come. Snow was falling out-doors. Katy could see the thick flakes go whirling past the window, but the sight did not chill her. It only made the room look warmer and more cosy. It was a pleasant room now. There was a bright fire in the grate. Everything was neat and orderly, the air was sweet with mignonette, from a little glass of flowers which stood on the table, and the Katy who lay in bed was a very different-looking Katy from the forlorn girl of two months ago. Cousin Helen's visit, though it lasted only one day, did great good.

'I wish I had something pretty to put into everybody's stocking,' she went on, wistfully; 'but I've only got the gloves for papa and these reins for Phil.' She took them from under her pillow as she spoke — gay, woollen affairs, with bells sewed

They both decided that it would do nicely for Clover

on here and there. She had knitted them herself, a very little bit at a time.

'There's my pink sash,' she said suddenly; 'I might give that to Clover. I only wore it once, you know, and I don't *think* I got any spots on it. Would you please fetch it and let me see, Aunt Izzie? It's in the top drawer.'

Aunt Izzie brought the sash. It proved to be quite fresh, and they both decided that it would do nicely for Clover.

'You know I shan't want sashes for ever so long,' said Katy, in rather a sad tone. 'And this is a beauty.'

When she spoke next, her voice was bright again.

'I wish I had something very nice for Elsie. Do you know, Aunt Izzie, I think Elsie is the dearest little girl that ever was.'

'I'm glad you've found it out,' said Aunt Izzie, who had always been specially fond of Elsie.

'What she wants most of all is a writing-desk,' continued Katy. 'And Johnnie wants a sled. But, oh dear! those are such big things. And I've only got two dollars and a quarter.'

Aunt Izzie marched out of the room without saying anything. When she came back she had something folded up in her hand.

'I didn't know what to give you for Christmas, Katy,' she said, 'so I thought I'd give you this, and let you choose for yourself. But if you've set your heart on getting presents for the children, perhaps you'd rather have it now.'

So saying, Aunt Izzie laid on the bed a crisp, new five-dollar note!

'How good you are!' cried Katy, flushed with pleasure. And indeed Aunt Izzie *did* seem to have grown wonderfully good lately.

Being now in possession of seven dollars and a quarter, Katy could afford to be gorgeously generous. She gave Aunt Izzie an exact description of the desk she wanted.

'It's no matter about its being very big,' said Katy, 'but it must have a blue velvet lining, and an ink-stand with a silver top. And please buy some little sheets of paper and envelopes, and a pen-handle; the prettiest you can find. Oh! and there must be a lock and key. Don't forget that, Aunt Izzie.'

'No, I won't. What else?'

'I'd like the sled to be green,' went on Katy, 'and to have a nice name. "Sky-Scraper" would be nice, if there was one. Johnnie saw a sled once called "Sky-Scraper", and she said it was splendid. And if there's money enough left, Auntie, won't you buy me a nice book for Dorry, and another for Cecy, and a silver thimble for Mary? Her old one is full of holes. Oh! and some candy. And something for Debby and Bridget — some little thing, you know. I think that's all!'

Was ever seven dollars and a quarter expected to do so much? Aunt Izzie must have been a witch indeed to make it hold out. But she did, and next day all the precious bundles came home. How Katy enjoyed untying the strings!

Everything was exactly right.

'There wasn't any "Sky-Scraper",' said Aunt Izzie, 'so I got "Snow-Skimmer" instead.'

'It's beautiful, and I like it just as well,' said Katy, contentedly.

These delightful secrets took up so much of her thoughts that Katy scarcely found time to wonder at the absence of the children, who generally haunted her room, but for three days they had hardly been seen. However, after supper they all came up in a body, looking very merry and as if they had been having a good time somewhere.

'You don't know what we've been doing,' began Philly.

'Hush, Phil!' said Clover, in a warning voice. Then she divided the stockings which she held in her hand. And everybody proceeded to hang them up.

Dorry hung his on one side of the fireplace, and John hers exactly opposite. Clover and Phil put theirs to hand side by side on two handles of the bureau.

'I'm going to put mine here, close to Katy, so that she can see it first thing in the morning,' said Elsie, pinning hers to the bed-post.

Then they all sat down round the fire to write their wishes on bits of paper, and see whether they would burn, or fly up the chimney. If they did the latter, it was a sign that Santa

Then they all sat down round the fire to write their wishes on bits of paper

Claus had them safe, and would bring the things wished for.

Pretty soon Aunt Izzie came in and swept them all off to bed.

'I know how it will be in the morning,' she said, 'you'll all be up and racing about as soon as it is light. So you must get your sleep now, if ever.'

After they had gone, Katy recollected that nobody had offered to hang a stocking up for her. She felt a little hurt when she thought of it. 'But I suppose they forgot,' she said to herself.

A little later papa and Aunt Izzie came in, and they filled the stockings. It was great fun. Each was brought to Katy, as she lay in bed, that she might arrange it as she liked.

The toes were stuffed with candy and oranges. Then came

[121]

the parcels, all shapes and sizes, tied in white paper, with ribbons, and labelled.

'What's that?' asked Dr. Carr, as Aunt Izzie rammed a long, narrow package into Clover's stocking.

'A nail-brush,' answered Aunt Izzie. 'Clover needed a new one.'

How papa and Katy laughed! 'I don't believe Santa Claus ever had such a thing before,' said Dr. Carr.

'He must be a very dirty old gentleman, then,' observed Aunt Izzie, grimly.

The desk and sled were too big to go into any stocking, so they were wrapped in paper and hung beneath the other things. Is was ten o'clock before all was done, and papa and Aunt Izzie went away. Katy lay a long time watching the queer shapes of the stocking-legs as they dangled in the firelight. Then she fell asleep.

It seemed only a minute before something touched her and woke her up. Behold, it was day-time, and there was Philly in his night-gown, climbing up on the bed to kiss her! The rest of the children, half-dressed, were dancing about with their stockings in their hands.

'Merry Christmas! Merry Christmas!' they cried. 'Oh Katy, such beautiful, *beautiful* things!'

'Oh!' shrieked Elsie, who at that moment spied her desk, 'Santa Claus *did* bring it, after all! Why, it's got "from Katy" written on it! Oh, Katy, it's so sweet, and I'm *so* happy!' and Elsie hugged Katy, and sobbed for pleasure.

But what was that strange thing beside the bed? Katy stared and rubbed her eyes. It certainly had not been there when she went to sleep. How had it come?

It was a little evergreen tree planted in a red flower-pot. The

[122]

It was a little evergreen tree planted in a red flower-pot

pot had stripes of gilt paper stuck on it, and gilt stars and
crosses, which made it look very gay. The boughs of the tree
were hung with oranges, and nuts, and shiny red apples, and
popcorn balls, and strings of bright berries. There were also
a number of little packages tied with blue and crimson ribbon,
and altogether the tree looked so pretty that Katy gave a cry
of delighted surprise.

'It's a Christmas-tree for you, because you're ill, you know!'
said the children, all trying to hug her at once.

'We made it ourselves,' said Dorry, hopping about on one
foot. 'I pasted the black stars on the pot.'

'And I popped the corn!' cried Philly.

'Do you like it?' asked Elsie, cuddling close to Katy. 'That's my present — that one tied with a green ribbon. I wish it was nicer! Don't you want to open them at once?'

Of course Katy wanted to. All sorts of things came out of the little bundles. The children had arranged every parcel themselves. No grown person had been allowed to help in the least.

Elsie's present was a pen-wiper, with a grey flannel kitten on it. Johnnie's, a doll's tea-tray of scarlet tin.

'Isn't it beau-ti-ful?' she said, admiringly.

Dorry's gift, I regret to say, was a huge red-and-yellow spider, which whirred wildly when waved at the end of its string.

'They didn't want me to buy it,' he said, 'but I did! I thought it would amuse you. Does it amuse you, Katy?'

'Yes, indeed,' said Katy, laughing and blinking as Dorry waved the spider to and fro before her eyes.

'You can play with it when we are not here and you're all alone, you know,' remarked Dorry, highly gratified.

'But you don't notice what the tree's standing upon,' said Clover.

It was a chair, a very large and curious one, with a long-cushioned back, which ended in a footstool.

'That's papa's present,' said Clover. 'See, it tips back so as to be just like a bed. And papa said he thinks pretty soon you can lie on it, in the window, where you can see us play.'

'Does he really?' said Katy, doubtfully. It still hurt her very much to be touched or moved.

'And see what's tied to the arm of the chair,' said Elsie.

It was a little silver bell, with 'Katy' engraved on the handle.

'Cousin Helen sent it. It's for you to ring when you want anybody to come,' explained Elsie.

'Does it amuse you, Katy?'

'How perfectly lovely everybody is!' said Katy, with grateful tears in her eyes.

That was a pleasant Christmas. The children declared it to be the nicest they had ever had. And though Katy couldn't quite say that, she enjoyed it too, and was very happy.

It was several weeks before she was able to use the chair, but when once she became accustomed to it, it proved very comfortable. Aunt Izzie would dress her in the morning, tip the chair back till it was on a level with the bed, and then, very gently and gradually, draw her over on to it. Wheeling across the room was always painful, but sitting in the window and looking out at the clouds, the people going by, and the children playing in the snow, was delightful. How delightful nobody knows, excepting those who, like Katy, have lain for months in bed, without a peep at the outside world. Every day she grew brighter and more cheerful.

* * * * *

It was one day about six weeks after this, when Clover and Elsie were busy downstairs, that they were startled by the sound of Katy's bell ringing in a sudden and agitated manner. Both ran up two steps at a time to see what was wanted.

Katy sat in her chair looking very much flushed and excited. 'Oh, girls!' she exclaimed, 'what do you think? I stood up!'

'What?' cried Clover and Elsie.

'I really did! I stood up on my feet! By myself!'

The others were too much astonished to speak, so Katy went on explaining.

'It was all at once, you see. Suddenly I had the feeling that if I tried I could, and almost before I thought, I *did* try, and there I was, up and out of the chair. Only I kept hold of the arm all the time! I don't know how I got back, I was so frightened. Oh, girls!' — and Katy buried her face in her hands.

'Do you think I shall ever be able to do it again?' she asked, looking up with wet eyes.

'Why, of course you will!' said Clover, while Elsie danced about, crying out anxiously: 'Be careful! Do be careful!'

Katy tried, but she could not move out of the chair at all. She began to wonder if she had dreamed the whole thing.

But next day, when Clover happened to be in the room, she heard a sudden exclamation, and turning, there stood Katy, absolutely on her feet.

[126]

'*Only I kept hold of the arm all the time!*'

'Papa! Papa!' shrieked Clover rushing downstairs. 'Dorry, John, Elsie — come! Come and see!'

Papa was out, but all the rest crowded up at once. This time Katy found no trouble in 'doing it again'. It seemed as if her will had been asleep, and now that it had waked up, the limbs recognised its orders and obeyed them.

When papa came in he was as much excited as any of the children. He walked round the chair, questioning Katy and making her stand up and sit down.

'Am I really going to get well?' she asked, almost in a whisper.

'Yes, my love, I think you are,' replied Dr. Carr, seizing Phil and giving him a toss into the air. None of the children

[127]

'There!' she said, 'now you're adorned'

had ever before seen papa behave so like a boy. But pretty soon, noticing Katy's burning cheeks and excited eyes, he calmed himself, sent the others all away, and sat down to soothe and quiet her with gentle words.

'I think it is coming, my darling,' he said, 'but it will take time, and you must have a great deal of patience.'

Her progress was slow, as Dr. Carr had predicted. At first she only stood on her feet a few seconds, then a minute, then five minutes, holding tightly all the while to the chair. After that she began to walk a step at a time, pushing a chair before her, as children do when they are learning the use of their feet. Clover and Elsie hovered about her as she moved, like anxious mammas. It was odd, and a little pitiful, to see tall Katy with

[128]

her feeble, unsteady progress and the active figures of the little sisters following her protectingly. But Katy did not consider it either odd or pitiful; to her it was simply delightful — the most delightful thing possible. No baby of a year old was ever prouder of his first steps than she.

Gradually she grew more daring and ventured on a bolder flight. Clover, running upstairs one day to her own room, stood transfixed at the sight of Katy sitting there, flushed, panting, but enjoying the surprise she caused.

'You see,' she explained in an apologizing tone, 'I was seized with a desire to explore. It is such a time since I saw any room but my own! But, oh dear, how long that hall is! I had forgotten it could be so long. I shall have to take a good rest before I go back.'

Katy did take a good rest, but she was very tired next day. The experiment, however, did no harm. In the course of two or three weeks she was able to walk all over the second storey.

By the end of August she was grown so strong that she began to talk about going downstairs. But papa said, 'Wait.'

'It will tire you much more than walking about on the level,' he explained; 'you had better put it off a little while — till you are quite sure of your feet.'

At last the great day came — the very ideal of a September day.

'Katy,' said Clover, as she came in from the garden with her hands full of flowers, 'that dress of yours is sweet. You never looked so nice before in your life!' And she stuck a beautiful carnation pink under Katy's breast-pin, and fastened another in her hair.

'There!' she said, 'now you're adorned. Papa is coming up in a few minutes to take you down.'

Just then Elsie and Johnnie came in. They had on their

[129]

best frocks. So had Clover. It was evidently a festival day to all the house. Cecy followed, invited over for the special purpose of seeing Katy walk downstairs. She, too, had on a new frock.

'How fine we are!' said Clover, as she noticed this magnificence. 'Turn round, Cecy — a panier, I do declare — and a sash! You are getting awfully grown-up, Miss Hall.'

'None of us will ever be so "grown-up" as Katy,' said Cecy, laughing.

And now papa appeared. Very slowly they all went downstairs, Katy leaning on papa, with Dorry on her other side and the girls behind, while Philly clattered ahead. And there were Debby and Bridget, the maids, and Alexander, peeping out of the kitchen door to watch her, and dear old Mary with her apron at her eyes, crying for joy.

'Oh, the front door is open!' said Katy, in a delighted tone. 'How nice! And what a pretty oil-cloth! That's new since I was here.'

'Don't stop to look at *that*!' cried Philly, who seemed in a great hurry about something. 'It isn't new. It's been there ever and ever so long! Come with me into the parlour instead.'

'Yes,' said papa; 'dinner isn't quite ready yet. You'll have time to rest a little after your walk downstairs. You have borne it admirably, Katy. Are you very tired?'

'Not a bit!' replied Katy, cheerfully. 'I could do it alone, I think. Oh! the bookcase door has been mended. How nice it looks!'

'Don't wait, oh, don't wait!' repeated Phil, in an agony of impatience.

So they moved on. Papa opened the parlour door. Katy took

one step into the room — then stopped. The colour flashed over her face, and she held by the door-knob to support herself. What was it that she saw?

Not merely the room itself, with its fresh muslin curtains and vases of flowers. Nor even the wide, beautiful window which faced directly toward the sun, or the inviting little couch and table which stood there, evidently for her. No, there was something else! The sofa was pulled out, and there upon it, supported by pillows, her bright eyes turned to the door, lay — Cousin Helen! When she saw Katy she held out her arms.

Clover and Cecy agreed afterward that they never were so frightened in their lives as at this moment; for Katy, forgetting her weakness, let go of papa's arm, and absolutely *ran* toward the sofa. 'Oh, Cousin Helen! Dear, dear Cousin Helen!' she cried. Then she tumbled down by the sofa somehow, the two pairs of arms and the two faces met, and for a moment or two not a word more was heard from anybody.

'Isn't it a nice surprise?' shouted Philly, turning a somersault by way of relieving his feelings, while John and Dorry executed a sort of war-dance round the sofa.

Phil's voice seemed to break the spell of silence, and a perfect hubbub of questions and exclamations began.

It appeared that this happy thought of getting Cousin Helen to the 'Celebration', was Clover's. She it was who had proposed it to papa, and made all the arrangements.

'Cousin Helen's going to stay three weeks this time — isn't that nice?' asked Elsie, while Clover anxiously questioned: 'Are you sure that you didn't suspect? Not the least bit?'

'No, indeed — not the least. How could I suspect anything so perfectly delightful?' And Katy gave Cousin Helen another rapturous kiss.

Such a short day that seemed! There was so much to see, to ask about, to talk over, that the hours flew, and evening dropped upon them all like another great surprise.

Cousin Helen was perhaps the happiest of the party. Besides the pleasure of knowing Katy to be almost well again, she had the additional enjoyment of seeing for herself how many changes for the better had taken place among the little cousins she loved so much.

To all the children, Katy was evidently the centre and the sun. They all revolved about her, and trusted her for everything. Cousin Helen looked on as Phil came in crying, after a hard tumble, and was consoled; as Johnnie whispered an important secret, and Elsie begged for help in her work. She saw Katy meet them all pleasantly and sweetly, without a bit of her old impetuous voice. And best of all, she saw the change in Katy's own face, the gentle expression of her eyes, the womanly look, the pleasant voice, the politeness, the tact in advising the others, without seeming to advise.

'Dear Katy,' she said, a day or two after her arrival, 'this visit is a great pleasure to me — you can't think how great. It is such a contrast to the last I made, when you were so sick, and everybody so sad. Do you remember?'

'Indeed I do. And how good you were, and how you helped me. I shall never forget that.'

'I'm glad. But what I could do was very little. You have been learning by yourself all this time. And, Katy darling, I want to tell you how pleased I am to see how bravely you have worked your way up. You have won the place, which I once told you an invalid should try to gain, of being to everybody "The Heart of the House".'

'Oh, Cousin Helen, don't!' said Katy, her eyes filling with

sudden tears. 'I haven't been brave. You can't think how badly I have behaved sometimes — how cross and ungrateful I am, and how stupid and slow. Every day I see things which ought to be done, and I don't do them. It's too delightful to have you praise me — but you mustn't. I don't deserve it.'

But although she said she didn't deserve it, I think that Katy did!

BLACK BEAUTY

by Anna Sewell

When I was young all my time was spent with my mother. In the day-time I ran by her side, and at night I lay down close by her. When it was hot, we used to stand by the pond in the shade of the trees, and when it was cold, we had a nice warm shed near the plantation.

As soon as I was old enough to eat grass, my mother used to go out to work in the daytime, and came back in the evening.

There were six young colts in the meadow beside me. They were older than I was; some were nearly as large as grown-up horses. I used to run with them, and had great fun. We used to gallop all together round and round the field, as hard as we could go. Sometimes we had rather rough play, for they would frequently bite and kick as well as gallop.

One day, when there was a good deal of kicking, my mother whinnied to me to come to her, and then she said:

'I wish you to pay attention to what I am going to say to you. The colts who live here are very good colts, but they are cart-horse colts, and, of course, they have not learned manners. You have been well bred and well born; your father has a great name in these parts, and your grandfather won the cup two years at the Newmarket races. Your grandmother had the sweetest temper of any horse I ever knew, and I think you have never seen me kick or bite. I hope you will grow up gentle and good, and never learn bad ways. Do your work with a good will, lift your feet up well when you trot, and never bite or kick, even in play.'

I have never forgotten my mother's advice; I knew she was a wise old horse, and our master thought a great deal of her. Her name was Duchess, but he often called her Pet.

When I was four years old, Squire Gordon came to look at me. He examined my eyes, my mouth, and my legs; he felt them all down, and then I had to walk and trot and gallop before him. He seemed to like me, and said, 'When he has been well broken in, he will do very well.' My master said he would break me in himself, as he should not like me to be frightened or hurt, and he lost no time about it, for the next day he began.

I had, of course, long been used to a halter and a headstall, and to be led about in the fields and lanes quietly, but now I was to have a bit and a bridle. My master gave me some oats as usual, and after a good deal of coaxing, he got the bit into my mouth, and the bridle fixed, but it was a nasty thing! Those who have never had a bit in their mouths cannot think how bad it feels. A great piece of cold, hard steel as thick as a man's finger to be pushed into your mouth, between the teeth and over the tongue, with the ends coming out at the corner of your mouth, and held fast there by straps over your head, under your throat, round your nose, and under your chin; so that no way in the world can you get rid of the nasty, hard thing.

Next came the saddle, but that was not half so bad. My master put it on my back very gently, whilst old Daniel held my head. He then made the girths fast under my body, patting and talking to me all the time. I had a few oats, then a little leading about, and this he did every day till I began to look for the oats and the saddle. At length, one morning, my master got on my back and rode me round the meadow on the soft grass. It certainly did feel queer, but I must say I felt rather proud to carry my master, and as he continued to ride me a little every day, I soon became accustomed to it.

The next unpleasant business was putting on the iron shoes; that, too, was very hard at first. My master went with me to the smith's forge, to see that I was not hurt or frightened. The blacksmith took my feet in his hand, one after the other, and cut away some of the hoof. It did not pain me, so I stood still on three legs till he had done them all. Then he took a piece of iron, the shape of my foot, and clapped it on, and drove some nails through the shoe into my hoof, so that the shoe was firmly on. My feet felt very stiff and heavy, but in time I got used to it.

And now, having got so far, my master went on to break me to harness; there were more new things to wear. First, a stiff heavy collar on my neck, and a bridle with great side-pieces called blinkers against my eyes, and blinkers indeed they were, for I could not see on either side, but only straight in front of me. Next there was a small saddle with a nasty stiff strap that went right under my tail; that was the crupper.

Master took me to the blacksmith

I hated the crupper — to have my long tail doubled up and poked through that strap was almost as bad as the bit. I never felt more like kicking, but of course I could not kick such a good master, and so in time I got used to everything, and could do my work as well as my mother.

Early in May there came a man from Squire Gordon's, who took me away to the Hall. My master said, 'Good-bye, Darkie. Be a good horse, and always do your best.' I could not say 'good-bye', so I put my nose into his hand. He patted me kindly, and I left my first home.

The stable into which I was taken was very roomy, with four good stalls; a large swinging window opened into the yard, which made it pleasant and airy.

The first stall was a large square one, shut in behind with a wooden gate; the others were common stalls, good stalls, but not nearly so large. It was called a loose box, because the horse that was put into it was not tied up, but left loose, to do as he liked. It is a great thing to have a loose box. In the stall next to mine stood a little fat grey pony, with a thick mane and tail, a very pretty head, and a pert little nose.

I put my head up to the iron rails at the top of my box, and said, 'How do you do? What is your name?'

He turned round as far as his halter would allow, held up his head, and said, 'My name is Merrylegs. Are you going to live next door to me in this box?'

I said, 'Yes.'

'Well, then,' he said, 'I hope you are good-tempered. I do not like anyone next door who bites.'

Just then a horse's head looked over from the stall beyond; the ears were laid back, and the eye looked rather ill-tempered. This was a tall chestnut mare, with a long handsome neck. She looked across to me and said: 'So it is you who have turned me out of my box. It is a very strange thing for a colt like you to come and turn a lady out of her own home.'

'I beg your pardon,' I said, 'I have turned no one out. The man who brought me put me here, and I had nothing to do with it. As to my being a colt, I am turned four years old, and am a grown-up horse. I never had words yet with horse or mare, and it is my wish to live at peace.'

'Well,' she said, 'we shall see; of course, I do not want to have words with a young thing like you.'

I said no more.

In the afternoon when she went out, Merrylegs told me all about it.

[141]

'The thing is this,' said Merrylegs. 'Ginger has a bad habit of biting and snapping. That is why they call her Ginger, and when she was in the loose box, she used to snap very much. One day she bit John the groom in the arm and made it bleed, and so Miss Flora and Miss Jessie, who are very fond of me, were afraid to come into the stable. They used to bring me nice things to eat, an apple or a carrot, or a piece of bread, but after Ginger stood in that box, they dare not come, and I missed them very much. I hope they will now come again, if you do not bite or snap.'

The next day I was brought out for my master. I remembered my mother's counsel and my good old master's, and I tried to do exactly what my new master wanted me to do. I found he was a very good rider, and thoughtful for his horse, too. When he came home, a lady was at the hall door as he rode up.

'Well, my dear,' she said, 'how do you like him?'

'He is exactly what John said,' he replied; 'a pleasanter creature I never wished to mount. What shall we call him?'

'Would you like Ebony?' said she; 'he is as black as ebony.'

'No, not Ebony.'

'Will you call him Blackbird, like your uncle's old horse?'

'No, he is far handsomer than old Blackbird ever was.'

'Yes,' she said, 'he is really quite a beauty, and he has such a sweet good-tempered face and such a fine intelligent eye — what do you say to calling him Black Beauty?'

'Black Beauty — why, yes, I think that is a very good name. If you like, it shall be his name,' and so it was.

A few days after this I had to go out with Ginger in the carriage. I wondered how we should get on together but, except for laying her ears back when I was led up to her, she

I tried to do exactly what he wanted me to do

behaved very well. She did her work honestly, and did her full share, and I never wish to have a better partner in double harness. When we came to a hill, instead of slackening her pace, she would throw her weight right into the collar, and pull away straight up. We had both the same sort of courage at our work, and John, the coachman, had oftener to hold us in than to urge us forward. He never had to use the whip with either of us. Then our paces were much the same, and I found it very easy to keep step with her when trotting, which made it pleasant, and master always liked it when we kept step well, and so did John. After we had been out two or three times together we grew quite friendly and sociable, which made me feel very much at home.

Our master had two other horses that stood in another stable. One was Justice, a roan cob, used for riding, or for the luggage cart; the other was an old brown hunter, named Sir Oliver. He was past work now, but was a great favourite with the master, who gave him the run of the park. Sometimes he did a little light carting on the estate, or carried one of the young ladies when they rode out with their father, for he was very gentle, and could be trusted with a child as much as Merrylegs. The cob was a strong, well-made, good-tempered horse, and we sometimes had a little chat in the paddock, but of course I could not be so intimate with him as with Ginger, who stood in the same stable.

The next time that Ginger and I were together in the paddock, she told me about her last home.

'I had a good master, and I was getting on very well, but his old groom left him, and a new one came. This man was as hard-tempered and hard-handed as Samson. He always spoke in a rough, impatient voice, and if I did not move in the stall the moment he wanted me, he would hit me above the hocks with his stable broom or the fork, whichever he might have in his hand. Everything he did was rough, and I began to hate him. He wanted to make me afraid of him, but I was too high-minded for that, and one day when he had aggravated me more than usual, I bit him, which of course put him in a great rage, and he began to hit me about the head with a riding whip. After that, he never dared to come into my stall again, either my heels or my teeth were ready for him, and he knew it. I was quite quiet with my master, but, of course, he listened to what the man said, and so I was sold again.

'The same dealer heard of me, and said he thought he knew one place where I should do well. " 'Twas a pity," he said,

We grew quite friendly

"that such a fine horse should go to the bad for want of a real good chance," and the end of it was that I came here not long before you did. But I had then made up my mind that men were my natural enemies, and that I must defend myself. Of course it is very different here, but who knows how long it will last? I wish I could think about things as you do, but I can't after all I have gone through.'

I was sorry for Ginger, but, of course, I knew very little, then, and I thought most likely she made the worst of it. However, I found that as the weeks went on, she grew much more gentle and cheerful, and had lost the watchful, defiant look that she used to turn on any strange person who came near her. ✻ ✻ ✻ ✻ ✻

One day late in the autumn, my master had a long journey to go on business. I was put into the dog-cart, and John went with his master. I always liked to go in the dog-cart. It was so light, and the high wheels ran along so pleasantly. There had been a great deal of rain, and now the wind was very high, and blew the dry leaves across the road in a shower. We went along merrily till we came to a toll-bar and a low wooden bridge. The river banks were rather high, and the bridge, instead of rising, went across just level, so that in the middle, if the river was full, the water would be nearly up to the wood-work and planks but, as there were good substantial rails on each side, people did not mind it.

The man at the gate said the river was rising fast, and he feared it would be a bad night. Many of the meadows were under water, and in one low part of the road the water was halfway up to my knees. However, the bottom was good, and master drove gently, so it was no matter.

When we got to the town, of course, I had a good feed, but, as the master's business engaged him a long time, we did not start for home till rather late in the afternoon. The wind was then much higher, and I heard the master say to John he had never been out in such a storm; and so I thought, as we went along the skirts of a wood, where the great branches were swaying about like twigs, and the rushing sound was terrible.

'I wish we were well out of this wood,' said my master.

'Yes, sir,' said John, 'it would be rather awkward if one of these branches came down upon us.'

The words were scarcely out of his mouth when there was a groan, and a crack, and a splitting sound, and tearing, crashing down amongst the other trees came an oak, torn up by the roots, and it fell right across the road just before us. I will

I was frightened

never say I was not frightened, for I was. I stopped still, and I believe I trembled. Of course I did not turn round or run away; I was not brought up to that. John jumped out and in a moment was at my head.

'That was a very near touch,' said my master; 'what's to be done now?'

'Well, sir, we can't drive over that tree nor yet get round it. There will be nothing for it but to go back to the four cross-ways, and it will be a good six miles before we get round to the wooden bridge again. It will make us late, but the horse is fresh.'

So back we went, and round by the cross-roads. But by the time we got to the bridge it was very nearly dark. We could just see that the water was over the middle of it but, as that happened sometimes when the floods were out, master did not stop. We were going along at a good pace, but the moment my feet touched the first part of the bridge, I felt sure there was something wrong. I dare not go forward, and I made a dead stop. 'Go on, Beauty,' said my master, and he gave me a touch with the whip, but I dare not stir. He gave me a sharp cut. I jumped, but I dare not go forward.

'There's something wrong, sir,' said John, and he sprang out of the dog-cart and came to my head and looked all about. He tried to lead me forward. 'Come on, Beauty, what's the matter?' Of course I could not tell him, but I knew very well that the bridge was not safe.

Just then the man at the toll-gate on the other side ran out of the house, waving a lantern about like one mad.

'Hoy, hoy, hoy, halloo, stop!' he cried.

'What's the matter?' shouted my master.

'The bridge is broken in the middle, and part of it is carried away. If you come on you'll be into the river.'

'Thank God!' said my master.

'You Beauty!' said John, and took the bridle and gently turned me round to the righthand road by the river side. The sun had set some time, the wind seemed to have lulled off after that furious blast which tore up the tree. It grew darker and darker, stiller and stiller. I trotted quietly along, the wheels hardly making a sound on the soft road. For a good while neither master nor John spoke, and then master began talking in a serious voice. I could not understand much of what they said, but I found they thought, if I had gone on as the master wanted me, most likely the bridge would have given way under us, and horse, chaise, master, and man would have fallen into the river; and as the current was flowing very strongly, and

'Stop!' he cried

there was no light and no help at hand, it was more than likely we should all have been drowned. Master said God had given men reason by which they could find out things for themselves, but he had given animals knowledge which did not depend on reason, and which was much more prompt and perfect in its way, and by which they had often saved the lives of men.

After this, it was decided by my master and mistress to pay a visit to some friends who lived about forty-six miles from our home, and John was to drive them. We stopped at the principal hotel, which was in the Market Place. It was a very large one, and we drove under an archway into a long yard, at the farther end of which were the stables and coach-houses. Two ostlers came to unharness Ginger and myself. The head ostler was a

[149]

pleasant, active little man, with a crooked leg, and a yellow striped waistcoat. I never saw a man unbuckle harness so quickly as he did, and with a pat and a good word he led me to a long stable, with six or eight stalls in it, and two or three horses. The other man brought Ginger. John stood by whilst we were rubbed down and cleaned. He also came in to look at us the last thing, and then the door was locked.

I cannot say how long I had slept, nor what time in the night it was, but I woke up feeling very uncomfortable, though I hardly knew why. I got up. The air seemed all thick and choking. I heard Ginger coughing, and one of the other horses seemed very restless. It was quite dark, and I could see nothing, but the stable seemed full of smoke, and I hardly knew how to breathe.

The trap door had been left open, and I thought that was the place it came through. I listened and heard a soft rushing sort of noise, and a low crackling and snapping. I did not know what it was, but there was something in the sound so strange, that it made me tremble all over. The other horses were now all awake. Some were pulling at their halters, others were stamping.

At last I heard steps outside, and the young ostler burst into the stable with a lantern, and began to untie the horses, and try to lead them out, but he seemed in such a hurry and so frightened himself that he frightened me still more. The first horse would not go with him. He tried the second and third, but they too would not stir. He came to me next and tried to drag me out of the stall by force. Of course, that was no use. He tried us all by turns and then left the stable.

No doubt we were very foolish, but danger seemed to be all round and there was nobody we knew to trust in, and all was

A fire broke out in the stable

strange and uncertain. The fresh air that had come in through the open door made it easier to breathe, but the rushing sound overhead grew louder, and as I looked upwards, through the bars of my empty rack, I saw a red light flickering on the wall. Then I heard a cry of 'Fire' outside, and the old ostler quietly and quickly came in. He got one horse out, and went to another, but the flames were playing round the trap door, and the roaring overhead was dreadful.

The next thing I heard was John's voice, quiet and cheery, as it always was.

'Come, my beauties, it is time for us to be off, so wake up and come along.' I stood nearest the door, so he came to me first, patting me as he came in.

'Come, Beauty, on with your bridle, my boy, we'll soon be out of this smother.' It was on in no time and he took the scarf off his neck, tied it lightly over my eyes, and patting and coaxing, he led me out of the stable. Safe in the yard, he slipped the scarf off my eyes, and shouted, 'Here, somebody! Take this horse while I go back for the other.'

A tall broad man stepped forward and took me, and John darted back into the stable. I set up a shrill whinny as I saw him go. Ginger told me afterwards that whinny was the best thing I could have done for her, for had she not heard me outside, she would never have had courage to come out.

There was much confusion in the yard — the horses being got out of other stables, and the carriages and gigs being pulled out of houses and sheds, lest the flames should spread farther. On the far side of the yard, windows were thrown up, and people were shouting all sorts of things; but I kept my eye fixed on the stable door, where the smoke poured out thicker than ever, and I could see flashes of red light. Presently I heard above all the stir and din a loud clear voice, which I knew was master's:

'John! Are you there?' There was no answer, but I heard a crash of something falling in the stable, and the next moment I gave a loud joyful neigh, for I saw John coming through the smoke, leading Ginger with him. She was coughing violently, and he was not able to speak.

'My brave lad!' said master, laying his hand on his shoulder, 'are you hurt?'

John shook his head, for he could not say a word.

'And now,' said master, 'when you have got your breath, John, we'll get out of this place as quickly as we can.'

We got out as fast as we could into the broad quiet Market

Place. The stars were shining, and except for the noise behind us, all was still. Master led the way to a large Hotel on the other side, and as soon as the ostler came, he said, 'John, I must now hasten to your mistress. I trust the horses entirely to you. Order whatever you think is needed,' and with that he was gone. The master did not run, but I never saw mortal man walk so fast as he did that night.

The rest of our journey was very easy, and a little after sunset we reached the house of my master's friend. We were taken into a clean, snug stable where there was a kind coachman, who made us very comfortable, and who seemed to think a good deal of John when he heard about the fire.

We stopped two or three days at this place, and then returned home. All went well on the journey. But we were glad to be in our own stable again.

* * * * *

One night, I had eaten my hay and was lying down in my straw fast asleep, when I was suddenly awakened by the stable bell ringing loudly. I heard the door of John's house open, and his feet running up to the Hall. He was back again in no time and unlocked the stable door and came in, calling out, 'Wake up, Black Beauty, you must go well now, if ever you did.'

Almost before I could think, he had got the saddle on my back and the bridle on my head. He just ran round for his coat, and then took me at a quick trot up to the Hall door. The Squire stood there with a lamp in his hand.

'Now, John,' he said, 'ride for your life — that is, for your mistress's life — there is not a moment to lose. Give this note

'Ride for your life . . .'

to Dr. White, give your horse a rest at the inn, and be back again as soon as you can.'

John said, 'Yes, sir,' and was on my back in a minute. The gardener who lived at the lodge had heard the bell ring, and was ready with the gate open, and away we went through the Park, and through the village, and down the hill till we came to the tollgate. John called very loud and thumped upon the door; the man was soon out and flung open the gate.

'Now,' said John, 'do you keep the gate open for the doctor. Here's the money,' and off we went again.

There was before us a long piece of level road by the riverside. John said to me, 'Now, Beauty, do your best,' and so I did. I wanted no whip nor spur, and for two miles I galloped as fast as I could lay my feet to the ground. I don't believe that my old grandfather who wo   the race at Newmarket could have gone faster. When we came to the bridge, John pulled me up a little and patted my neck. 'Well done, Beauty! Good old fellow,' he said. He would have let me go slower, but my spirit was up, and I was off again as fast as before. The air was frosty, the moon was bright, and it was very pleasant. We came through a village, then through a dark wood, then uphill, then downhill, till after an eight miles' run we came to the town, through the streets and into the Market Place. It was all quite still except for the clatter of my feet on the stones — everybody was asleep. The church clock struck three as we drew up at Doctor White's door. John rang the bell twice, and then knocked at the door like thunder. A window was thrown up, and Doctor White, in his nightcap, put his head out and said, 'What do you want?'

'Mrs. Gordon is very ill, sir. Master wants you to go at once, he thinks she will die if you cannot get there — here is a note.'

'Wait,' he said, 'I will come.'

He shut the window and was soon at the door.

'The worst of it is,' he said, 'that my horse has been out all day and is quite done up. My son has just been sent for, and he has taken the other. What is to be done? Can I have your horse?'

'He has come at a gallop nearly all the way, sir, and I was to give him a rest here; but I think my master would not be against it if you think fit, sir.'

'All right,' he said, 'I will soon be ready.'

John stood by me and stroked my neck. I was very hot. The doctor came out with his riding whip.

The doctor appeared at the window

'You need not take that, sir,' said John, 'Black Beauty will go till he drops. Take care of him, sir, if you can. I should not like any harm to come to him.'

'No! no! John,' said the doctor, 'I hope not,' and in a minute we had left John far behind.

I will not tell about our way back. The doctor was a heavier man than John, and not so good a rider; however, I did my very best. The man at the toll-gate had it open. When we came to the hill, the doctor drew me up. 'Now, my good fellow,' he said, 'take some breath.' I was glad he did, for I was nearly spent, but that breathing helped me on, and soon we were in the Park. Little Joe, the new stable-boy, was at the lodge gate, my master was at the Hall door, for he had heard us

He rubbed my legs and my chest

coming. He spoke not a word. The doctor went into the house
with him, and Joe led me to the stable. I was glad to get home,
and my legs shook under me, and I could only stand and pant.
I had not a dry hair on my body, the water ran down my legs,
and I steamed all over — Joe used to say, like a pot on the fire.
Poor Joe! He was young and small, and as yet he knew very
little, but I am sure he did the very best he knew. He rubbed
my legs and my chest, but he did not put my warm cloth on me.
He thought I was so hot I should not like it. Then he gave me
a pail full of water to drink. It was cold and very good, and
I drank it all. Then he gave me some hay and some corn,
and thinking he had done right, he went away. Soon I began
to shake and tremble, and turned deadly cold, my legs ached,

my loins ached, and my chest ached, and I felt sore all over. Oh, how I wished for my warm thick cloth as I stood and trembled. I wished for John, but he had eight miles to walk, so I lay down in my straw and tried to go to sleep. After a long while I heard John at the door. I gave a low moan, for I was in a great pain. He was at my side in a moment, stooping down by me. I could not tell him how I felt, but he seemed to know it all. He covered me up with two or three warm cloths, and then ran to the house for some hot water. He made me some warm gruel, which I drank, and then I think I went to sleep.

John seemed to be very much put out. I heard him say to himself, over and over again, 'Stupid boy! stupid boy! no cloth put on, and I dare say the water was cold, too; boys are no good,' but Joe was a good boy after all.

I was now very ill; a strong inflammation had attacked my lungs, and I could not draw my breath without pain. John nursed me night and day. He would get up two or three times in the night to come to me; my master, too, often came to see me. 'My poor Beauty,' he said one day, 'my good horse, you saved your mistress's life.' I was very glad to hear that, for it seems the doctor had said if we had been a little longer it would have been too late.

Ginger and Merrylegs had been moved into the other stable so that I might be quiet, for the fever made me very quick of hearing. Any little noise seemed quite loud, and I could tell everyone's footsteps going to and from the house. I knew all that was going on. One night John had to give me a draught. The medicine did well and sent me to sleep, and in the morning I felt much better.

John nursed me night and day

I had now lived in this happy place for three years, but sad changes were about to come over us. We heard from time to time that our mistress was ill. The doctor was often at the house, and the master looked grave and anxious. Then we heard that she must leave her home at once, and go to a warm country for two or three years. The news fell upon the household like the tolling of a death-bell. Everybody was sorry, but the master began directly to make arrangements for breaking up his establishment and leaving England. We used to hear it talked about in our stable; indeed nothing else was talked about. Then we heard what had been arranged for us. Master had sold Ginger and me to his old friend, the Earl of W - - - - - for he thought we should have a good place there.

Merrylegs he had given to the Vicar, who was wanting a pony for his wife, on the condition that he should never be sold, and when he was past work that he should be shot and buried.

Joe was engaged to take care of him, and to help in the house, so I thought that Merrylegs was well off. John had the offer of several good places, but he said he should wait a little and look round.

The evening before they left, the master came into the stable to give some directions, and to give his horses the last pat. He seemed very low-spirited; I knew that by his voice. I believe we horses can tell more by the voice than many men can.

'Have you decided what to do, John?' he said. 'I find you have not accepted either of these offers.'

'No, sir, I have made up my mind that if I could get a situation with some first-rate colt-breaker and horse-trainer, it would be the right thing for me. Many young animals are frightened and spoiled by wrong treatment, which need not be if the right man took them in hand. I always get on well with horses, and if I could help some of them to a fair start, I should feel as if I was doing something good. What do you think of it, sir?'

'I don't know a man anywhere,' said master, 'that I should think so suitable for it as yourself. You understand horses, and somehow they understand you, and in time you might set up for yourself. I think you could not do better. If in any way I can help you, write to me. I shall speak to my agent in London, and leave your character with him.'

Master gave John the name and address, and then he thanked him for his long and faithful service, but that was too much for John. 'Pray don't, sir, I can't bear it. You and my dear mistress have done so much for me that I could never repay it,

Master came down the steps carrying the mistress in his arms

but we shall never forget you, sir, and please God we may some day see mistress back again like herself. We must keep hope, sir.' Master gave John his hand, but he did not speak, and they both left the stable.

The last sad day had come. The footman and the heavy luggage had gone off the day before, and there were only master and mistress and her maid. Ginger and I brought the carriage up to the Hall door for the last time. The servants brought out cushions and rugs and many other things, and when all were arranged, master came down the steps carrying the mistress in his arms (I was on the side next the house, and could see all that went on). He placed her carefully in the carriage, while the house servants stood round crying.

[161]

'Good-bye, again,' he said. 'We shall not forget any of you,' and he got in. 'Drive on, John.'

Joe jumped up beside him and we trotted slowly through the Park, and through the village, where the people were standing at their doors to have a last look and to say 'God bless them.'

When we reached the railway station, I think mistress walked from the carriage to the waiting-room. I heard her say in her own sweet voice, 'Good-bye, John; God bless you.' I felt the rein twitch, but John made no answer; perhaps he could not speak. As soon as Joe had taken the things out of the carriage, John called him to stand by the horses, while he went on to the platform. Poor Joe! he stood close up to our heads to hide his tears. Very soon the train came puffing up into the station. Then two or three minutes, and the doors were slammed to. The guard whistled and the train glided away, leaving behind it only clouds of white smoke, and some very heavy hearts.

When it was quite out of sight, John came back.

'We shall never see her again,' he said; 'never.' He took the reins, mounted the box, and with Joe drove slowly home; but it was not our home now.

* * * * *

The next morning after breakfast Joe put Merrylegs into the mistress's low chaise to take him to the Vicarage. He came first and said good-bye to us, and Merrylegs neighed to us from the yard. Then John put the saddle on Ginger and the leading-rein on me, and rode us across the country about fifteen miles to Earlshall Park, where the Earl of W ----- lived. There was a very fine house, and a great deal of stabling, yet it was destined to be the scene of some alarming and un-happy experiences for both Ginger and myself.

Early in the spring, Lord W - - - - - and part of his family went up to London, taking York, the head coachman, with them. Ginger and I and some other horses were left at home, and the head groom was left in charge.

The Lady Harriet, who remained at the Hall, was a great invalid, and never went out in the carriage, and the Lady Anne preferred riding on horseback with her brother or cousins. She was a perfect horsewoman, and as gay and gentle as she was beautiful. She chose me for her horse, and named me 'Black Auster'! I enjoyed these rides very much in the clear, cold air, sometimes with Ginger, sometimes with Lizzie. This Lizzie was a bright bay mare, almost thoroughbred, and a great favourite with the gentlemen, on account of her fine action and lively spirit; but Ginger, who knew more of her than I did, told me she was rather nervous.

There was a gentleman of the name of Blantyre staying at the Hall. He always rode Lizzie, and praised her so much that one day Lady Anne ordered the side-saddle to be put on her, and the other saddle on me. When we came to the door the gentleman seemed very uneasy.

'How is this?' he said; 'are you tired of your good Black Auster?'

'Oh! no, not at all,' she replied; 'but I am amiable enough to let you ride him for once, and I will try your charming Lizzie. You must confess that in size and appearance she is far more like a lady's horse than my own favourite.'

'Do let me advise you not to mount her,' he said, 'she is a charming creature, but she is too nervous for a lady. I assure you she is not perfectly safe.'

'My dear cousin,' said Lady Anne, laughing, 'pray do not trouble your good careful head about me. I have been a horse-woman ever since I was a baby, and I intend to try this Lizzie that you gentlemen are so fond of. So please help me to mount like the good friend you are.'

There was no more to be said. He placed her carefully in the saddle, looked to the bit and curb, gave the reins gently into her hand, and then mounted me. Just as we were moving off, a footman came out with a slip of paper from the Lady Harriet — 'Would they ask this question for her at Dr. Ashley's, and bring the answer?'

The village was about a mile off, and the doctor's house was the last in it. We went along gaily enough till we came to his gate. There was a short drive up to the house between tall evergreens. Blantyre alighted at the gate, and was going to open it for Lady Anne, but she said, 'I will wait for you here, and you can hang Auster's rein on the gate.'

He looked at her doubtfully — 'I will not be five minutes,' he said.

'Oh, do not hurry yourself; Lizzie and I shall not run away from you.'

He hung my rein on one of the iron spikes, and was soon hidden amongst the trees. Lizzie was standing quietly by the side of the road a few paces off with her back to me. My young mistress was sitting easily with a loose rein, humming a little song. I listened to my rider's footsteps until they reached the house, and heard him knock at the door. There was a meadow on the opposite side of the road, the gate of which stood open. Just then some cart-horses and several young colts came trotting out in a very disorderly manner, whilst a boy behind was cracking a great whip. The colts were wild and frolicsome,

[164]

and one of them bolted across the road, and blundered up against Lizzie's hind legs; and whether it was the stupid colt, or the loud cracking of the whip, or both together I cannot say, but she gave a violent kick, and dashed off into a headlong gallop. It was so sudden that Lady Anne was nearly unseated, but she soon recovered herself. I gave a loud shrill neigh for help. Again and again I neighed, pawing the ground impatiently, and tossing my head to get the rein loose. I had not long to wait. Blantyre came running to the gate. He looked anxiously about, and just caught sight of the flying figure, now far away on the road. In an instant he sprang to the saddle. I needed no whip or spur, for I was as eager as my rider; he saw this, and giving me a free rein, and leaning a little forward, we dashed after them.

For about a mile and a half the road ran straight, and then bent to the right, after which it divided into two roads. Long before we came to the bend she was out of sight. Which way had she turned? A woman was standing at her garden gate, shading her eyes with her hand, and looking eagerly up the road. Scarcely drawing the rein, Blantyre shouted, 'Which way?' 'To the right,' cried the woman pointing with her hand, and away we went up the right-hand road. Then for a moment we caught sight of her; another bend and she was hidden again. Several times we caught glimpses and then lost them. We scarcely seemed to gain ground upon them at all. An old road-mender was standing near a heap of stones — his shovel dropped and his hands raised. As we came near he made a sign to speak. Blantyre drew the rein a little. 'To the common, to the common, sir; she has turned off there.' I knew this common very well. It was for the most part very uneven ground, covered with heather and dark green furze-bushes,

I gathered myself well together and with one determined leap cleared both dyke and bank

with here and there a scrubby old thorn-tree. There were also open spaces of fine short grass, with ant-hills and mole-turns everywhere, the worst place I ever knew for a headlong gallop.

We had hardly turned on the common, when we caught sight again of the green habit flying on before us. My lady's hat was gone, and her long brown hair was streaming behind her. Her head and body were thrown back, as if she were pulling with all her remaining strength, and as if that strength were nearly exhausted. It was clear that the roughness of the ground had very much lessened Lizzie's speed, and there seemed a chance that we might overtake her.

Whilst we were on the high-road, Blantyre had given me my head, but now with a light hand and a practised eye he

There were two men who, seeing Lizzy riderless, left their work to catch her

guided me over the ground in such a masterly manner that my pace was scarcely slackened, and we were decidedly gaining on them.

About halfway across the heath there had been a wide dyke recently cut, and the earth from the cutting was cast up roughly on the other side. Surely this would stop them. But no; with scarcely a pause, Lizzie took the leap, stumbled among the rough clods, and fell. Blantyre groaned, 'Now, Auster, do your best!' He gave me a steady rein, I gathered myself well together, and with one determined leap cleared both dyke and bank.

Motionless among the heather, with her face to the earth, lay my poor young mistress. Blantyre kneeled down and called her name — there was no sound. Gently he turned her face

[167]

upwards; it was ghastly white, and the eyes were closed. 'Annie, dear Annie, do speak!' but there was no answer. He unbuttoned her habit, loosened her collar, felt her hands and wrists, then started up and looked wildly round him for help.

At no great distance there were two men cutting turf, who, seeing Lizzie wild without a rider, left their work to catch her.

Blantyre's halloo soon brought them to the spot. The foremost man seemed much troubled at the sight, and asked what he could do.

'Can you ride?'

'Well, sir, I bean't much of a horseman, but I'd risk my neck for the Lady Anne. She was uncommon good to my wife in the winter.'

'Then mount this horse, my friend; your neck will be quite safe, and ride to the doctor's, and ask him to come instantly. Then on to the Hall — tell them all that you know, and bid them send me the carriage with Lady Anne's maid, and help. I shall stay here.'

'All right, sir, I'll do my best, and I pray God the dear young lady may open her eyes soon.' Then seeing the other man, he called out, 'Here, Joe, run for some water, and tell my missis to come as quick as she can to the Lady Anne.'

He then somehow scrambled into the saddle, and with a 'Gee up' and a clap on my sides with both his legs, he started on his journey, making a little circuit to avoid the dyke.

I shook him as little as I could help, but once or twice on the rough ground he called out, 'Steady! Woah! Steady.' On the high-road, we were all right, and at the doctor's and the Hall, he did his errand like a good man and true. They asked him in to take a drop of something. 'No! no,' he said, 'I'll be back to 'em again by a short cut through the fields, and be there afore the carriage.'

There was a great deal of hurry and excitement after the news became known. I was just turned into my box, the saddle and bridle were taken off, and a cloth thrown over me.

Ginger was saddled and sent off in great haste for Lord George, and I soon heard the carriage roll out of the yard.

It seemed a long time before Ginger came back, and before we were left alone, and then she told me all that she had seen.

'I can't tell much,' she said; 'we went at a gallop nearly all the way, and got there just as the doctor rode up. There was a woman sitting on the ground with the lady's head in her lap. The doctor poured something into her mouth, but all that I heard was "she is not dead". Then I was led off by a man to a little distance. After a while she was taken to the carriage, and we came home together. I heard my master say to a gentleman who stopped him to inquire, that he hoped no bones were broken, but that she had not spoken yet.'

When Lord George took Ginger for hunting, York shook his head. He said it ought to be a steady hand to train a horse for the first season, and not a random rider like Lord George.

Ginger used to like it very much, but sometimes when she came back, I could see that she had been very much strained, and now and then she gave a short cough. She had too much spirit to complain, but I could not help feeling anxious about her.

Two days after the accident, Blantyre paid me a visit; he patted me and praised me very much. He told Lord George that he was sure the horse knew of Anne's danger as well as he did. 'I could not have held him in, if I would,' said he; 'she ought never to ride any other horse.' I found by their conversation that my young mistress was now out of danger, and would soon be able to ride again.

I must now say a little about Reuben Smith, who was left in charge of the stables when York went to London. No one more thoroughly understood his business than he did, and when he was all right there could not be a more faithful or valuable man. He was gentle and very clever in his management of horses, and could doctor them almost as well as a farrier, for he had lived two years with a veterinary surgeon. He was a first-rate driver. He could take a four-in-hand, or a tandem, as easily as a pair. He was a handsome man, a good scholar, and had very pleasant manners. I believe everybody liked him, and certainly the horses did. The only wonder was that he should be in an under situation, and not in the place of a head coachman like York, but he had one great fault, and that was the love of drink. He was not like some men, always at it; he used to keep steady for weeks or months together, and then he would break out and have a 'bout' of it, as York called it, and be a disgrace to himself, a terror to his wife, and a nuisance to all who had to do with him. He was, however, so useful that two or three times York had hushed the matter up, and kept it from the Earl's knowledge. But one night, when Reuben had to drive a party home from a ball, he was so drunk that he could not hold the reins, and a gentleman of the party had to mount the box and drive the ladies home. Of course, this could not be hidden, and Reuben was at once dismissed. His poor wife and little children had to turn out of the pretty cottage by the Park gate, and go where they could. I was told all this, for it had happened a good while ago; but shortly before Ginger and I came, Smith had been taken back again. York had interceded for him with the Earl, who was very kind-

He was so drunk that he had to be dismissed

hearted, and the man had promised faithfully that he would never taste another drop as long as he lived there. He had kept his promise so well that York thought he might be safely trusted to fill his place while he was away, and he was so clever and honest that no one else seemed so well fitted for it.

It was now early in April, and the family was expected home some time in May. The light brougham was to be freshly done up, and as Colonel Blantyre was obliged to return to his regiment, it was arranged that Smith should drive him to town in it, and ride back. For this purpose, he took the saddle with him, and I was chosen for the journey. At the station the Colonel put some money into Smith's hand and bid him good-bye, saying, 'Take care of your young mistress, Reuben, and don't let Black Auster be hacked about by any random young prig that wants to ride him — keep him for the lady.'

We left the carriage at the maker's, and Smith rode me to the White Lion, and ordered the ostler to feed me well and have me ready for him at four o'clock. A nail in one of my front shoes had started as I came along, but the ostler did not notice it till just about four o'clock. Smith did not come into the yard till five, and then he said he should not leave till six, as he had met with some old friends. The man then told him of the nail, and asked if he should have the shoe looked to.

'No,' said Smith, 'that will be all right till we get home.'

He spoke in a very loud off-hand way, and I thought it very unlike him not to see about the shoe, as he was generally wonderfully particular about loose nails in our shoes. He did not come at six, nor seven, nor eight, and it was nearly nine o'clock before he called for me, and then it was with a loud, rough voice. He seemed in a very bad temper, and abused the ostler, though I could not tell what for.

The landlord stood at the door and said, 'Have a care, Mr. Smith!' but he answered angrily with an oath; and almost before he was out of the town he began to gallop, frequently giving me a sharp cut with his whip, though I was going at full speed. The moon had not yet risen, and it was very dark. The roads were stony, having been recently mended. Going over them at this pace, my shoe became looser, and when we were near the turnpike gate it came off.

If Smith had been in his right senses, he would have been sensible of something wrong in my pace, but he was too madly drunk to notice anything.

Beyond the turnpike was a long piece of road, upon which fresh stones had just been laid, large sharp stones, over which

[172]

Smith had met with some old friends

no horse could be driven quickly without risk of danger. Over this road, with one shoe gone, I was forced to gallop at my fastest speed, my rider meanwhile cutting into me with his whip, and with wild curses urging me to go still faster. Of course, my shoeless foot suffered dreadfully. The hoof was broken and split down to the very quick, and the inside was terribly cut by the sharpness of the stones.

This could not go on; no horse could keep his footing under such circumstances — the pain was too great. I stumbled, and fell with violence on both my knees. Smith was flung off by my fall, and owing to the speed I was going at, he must have fallen with great force. I soon recovered my feet and limped to the side of the road, where it was free from stones. The moon

I heard at a great distance the sound of a horse's feet

had just risen above the hedge, and by its light I could see
Smith lying a few yards beyond me. He did not rise, he made
one slight effort to do so, and then there was a heavy groan.
I could have groaned, too, for I was suffering intense pain both
from my foot and knees, but horses are used to bearing their
pain in silence. I uttered no sound, but I stood there and listened. One more heavy groan from Smith; but though he now
lay in the full moonlight, I could see no motion. I could do
nothing for him nor myself, but, oh! how I listened for the
sound of horse, or wheels, or footsteps. The road was not much
frequented, and at this time of the night we might stay for
hours before help came to us. I stood watching and listening.
It was a calm, sweet April night. There were no sounds, but

a few low notes of a nightingale, and nothing moved but the white clouds near the moon, and a brown owl that flitted over the hedge. It made me think of the summer nights long ago, when I used to lie beside my mother in the green, pleasant meadow.

* * * * *

It must have been nearly midnight when I heard at a great distance the sound of a horse's feet. Sometimes the sound died away, then it grew clearer again and nearer. The road to Earlshall led through plantations that belonged to the Earl. The sound came from that direction, and I hoped it might be someone coming in search of us. As the sound came nearer and nearer, I was almost sure I could distinguish Ginger's step. A little nearer still, and I could tell she was in the dogcart. I neighed loudly, and was overjoyed to hear an answering neigh from Ginger, and men's voices. They came over and stopped at the dark figure that lay upon the ground.

One of the men jumped out and stooped down over it. 'It is Reuben!' he said, 'and he does not stir!'

The other man followed and bent over him. 'He's dead,' he said; 'feel how cold his hands are.'

They raised him up, but there was no life, and his hair was soaked with blood. They laid him down again, and came and looked at me. They soon saw my cut knees.

'Why, the horse has been down and thrown him! Who would have thought the black horse would have done that? Nobody thought he could fall. Reuben must have been lying here for hours! Odd, too, that the horse has not moved from the place.'

Robert then attempted to lead me forward. I made a step, but almost fell again.

'Hallo! He's bad in his foot as well as his knees; look here — his hoof is cut all to pieces, he might well come down, poor fellow! I tell you what, Ned, I'm afraid it hasn't been all right with Reuben. Just think of him riding a horse over these stones without a shoe! Why, if he had been in his right senses, he would just as soon have tried to ride him over the moon. I'm afraid it has been the old thing over again. Poor Susan! She looked awfully pale when she came to my house to ask if he had not come home. She made believe she was not a bit anxious, and talked of a lot of things that might have kept him. But for all that, she begged me to go and meet him — but what must we do? There's the horse to get home as well as the body — and that will be no easy matter.'

Then followed a conversation between them, till it was agreed that Robert, as the groom, should lead me, and that Ned must take the body. It was a hard job to get it into the dog-cart, for there was no one to hold Ginger, but she knew as well as I did what was going on, and stood as still as a stone.

Ned started off very slowly with his sad load, and Robert came and looked at my foot again. Then he took his handkerchief and bound it closely round, and so he led me home. I shall never forget that night walk; it was more than three miles. Robert led me on very slowly and I limped and hobbled on as well as I could with great pain. I am sure he was sorry for me, for he often patted and encouraged me, talking to me in a pleasant voice.

At last I reached my own box, and had some corn, and after Robert had wrapped up my knees in wet cloths, he tied up my foot in a bran poultice to draw out the heat and cleanse it before the horse doctor saw it in the morning, and I managed to get myself down on the straw, and slept in spite of the pain.

[176]

The next day, after the farrier had examined my wounds, he said he hoped the joint was not injured, and if so, I should not be spoiled for work, but I should never lose the blemish. I believe they did the best to make a good cure, but it was a long and painful one. Proud flesh, as they called it, came up in my knees, and was burnt out with caustic, and when at last it was healed, they put a blistering fluid over the front of both knees to bring all the hair off. They had some reason for this, and I suppose it was all right.

* * * * *

As soon as my knees were sufficiently healed, I was turned into a small meadow for a month or two. No other creature was there, and though I enjoyed the liberty and the sweet grass, yet I had been so long used to society that I felt very lonely. Ginger and I had become fast friends, and now I missed her company extremely. I often neighed when I heard horses' feet passing in the road, but I seldom got an answer, till one morning the gate was opened, and who should come in but dear old Ginger. The man slipped off her halter and left her there. With a joyful whinny I trotted up to her. We were both glad to meet, but I soon found that it was not for our pleasure that she was brought to be with me. Her story was that she had been ruined by hard riding, and was now turned off to see what rest would do.

Lord George was young and would take no warning; he was a hard rider, and would hunt whenever he could get the chance, quite careless of his horse. Soon after I left the stable there was a steeplechase, and he determined to ride. Though the groom told him she was a little strained, and was not fit for the race, he did not believe it, and, on the day of the race, urged Ginger to keep up with the foremost riders. With her high spirits she strained herself to the utmost. She came in with the first three horses, but her wind was touched, beside which, he was too heavy for her, and her back was strained. 'And so,' she said, 'here we are — ruined in the prime of our youth and strength — you by a drunkard, and I by a fool; it is very hard.' We both felt it ourselves that we were not what we had been. However, that did not spoil the pleasure we had in each other's company. We did not gallop about as we once did, but we used to feed and lie down together, and stand for hours under one of the shady lime trees with our heads close to each other. And so we passed our time till the family returned from town.

One day we saw the Earl come into the meadow, and York was with him. Seeing who it was, we stood still under our lime tree and let them come up to us. They examined us carefully. The Earl seemed much annoyed.

'There is three hundred pounds flung away for no earthly use,' said he. 'The mare shall have a twelve months' run, and we shall see what that will do for her; but the black one, he must be sold. It's a great pity, but I could not have knees like these in my stables.'

After this they left us.

'They'll soon take you away,' said Ginger, 'and I shall lose the only friend I have, and most likely we shall never see each other again. It's a hard world!'

About a week after this, Robert came into the field with a halter, which he slipped over my head and led me away. My new master's name was Jeremiah Barker, but as everyone called him Jerry, I shall do the same. Polly, his wife, was just

They were a wonderful family

as good a match as a man could have. She was a plump, trim tidy little woman, with smooth dark hair, dark eyes, and a merry little mouth. Their boy was nearly twelve years old, a tall, frank, good-tempered lad, and little Dorothy (Dolly they called her) was her mother over again, at eight years old. They were all wonderfully fond of each other; I never knew such a happy, merry family before or since. Jerry had a cab of his own, and two horses, which he drove and attended to himself. His other horse was a tall, white, rather large-boned animal, called Captain. He was old now, but when he was young he must have been splendid.

The next morning, when I was well groomed, Polly and Dolly came into the yard to see me, and make friends. Harry

[179]

had been helping his father since early morning, and had stated his opinion that I should turn out a 'regular brick'. Polly brought me a slice of apple and Dolly a piece of bread, and made as much of me as if I had been the 'Black Beauty' of olden time. It was a great treat to be petted again, and talked to in a gentle voice, and I let them see as well as I could that I wished to be friendly. Polly thought I was very handsome, and a great deal too good for a cab, if it was not for the broken knees.

'Of course, there's no one to tell us whose fault that was,' said Jerry, 'and as long as I don't know, I shall give him the benefit of the doubt; for a firmer, neater stepper I never rode. We'll call him "Jack" after the old one — shall we, Polly?'

'Do,' she said, 'for I like to keep a good name going.'

Captain went out in the cab all the morning. Harry came in after school to feed me and give me water. In the afternoon I was put into the cab. Jerry took much pains to see if the collar and bridle fitted comfortably.

After driving through a side street we came to the large cabstand. On one side of this wide street were high houses with wonderful shop-fronts, and on the other was an old church and churchyard surrounded by iron palisades. Alongside these iron rails a number of cabs were drawn up, waiting for passengers; bits of hay were lying about on the ground; some of the men were standing together talking; and one or two were feeding their horses with bits of hay, and a drink of water. We pulled up in the rank at the back of the last cab.

The first week of my life as a cab horse was very trying. I had never been used to London, and the noise, the hurry, the crowds of horses, carts and carriages that I had to make my way through made me feel anxious and harassed, but

It was Ginger, but how changed!

I soon found that I could perfectly trust my driver, and then I made myself easy and got used to it.

* * * * *

One day, whilst our cab and many others were waiting outside one of the parks, where music was playing, a shabby old cab drove up beside ours. The horse was an old worn-out chestnut, with an ill-kept coat and bones that showed plainly through it. The knees knuckled over, and the forelegs were very unsteady. I had been eating some hay, and the wind rolled a little lock of it that way, and the poor creature put out her long thin neck and picked it up, and then turned round and looked about for more. There was a hopeless look in the dull eye that I could not help noticing, and then, as I was thinking where I had seen that horse before, she looked full at me and said, 'Black Beauty, is that you?'

It was Ginger, but how changed! The beautifully arched and glossy neck was now straight, and lank, and fallen in, the clean straight legs and delicate fetlocks were swelled; the joints were grown out of shape with hard work; the face, that was once so full of spirit and life, was now full of suffering, and I could tell by the heaving of her sides, and her frequent cough, how bad her breathing was.

Our drivers were standing together a little way off, so I sidled up to her a step or two, that we might have a little quiet talk. It was a sad tale that she had to tell.

After a twelve-months' run off at Earlshall, she was considered to be fit for work again, and was sold to a gentleman. For a little while she got on very well, but after a longer gallop than usual, the old strain returned, and after being rested and doctored, she was again sold. In this way she changed hands several times, but always getting lower down.

'And so at last,' said she, 'I was bought by a man who keeps a number of cabs and horses, and lets them out. You look well off, and I am glad of it, but I could not tell you what my life has been. When they found out my weakness, they said I was not worth what they gave for me, and that I must go into one of the low cabs, and just be used up; that is what they are doing, whipping and working with never one thought of what I suffer — they paid for me, and must get it out of me, they say. The man who hires me now pays a great deal of money to the owner every day, and so he has to get it out of me, too; and so it's all the week round and round, with never a Sunday rest.'

I said, 'You used to stand up for yourself if you were ill-used.'

'Ah!' she said, 'I did once, but it's no use. Men are strongest, and if they are cruel and have no feeling, there is nothing that we can do, but just bear it, bear it on and on to the end. I wish the end was come, I wish I was dead. I have seen dead horses, and I am sure they do not suffer pain. I wish I may drop down dead at my work, and not be sent off to the knacker's.'

I was very much troubled, and I put my nose up to hers, but I could say nothing to comfort her. I think she was pleased to see me, for she said, 'You are the only friend I ever had.'

Just then her driver came up, and with a tug at her mouth, backed her out of the line and drove off, leaving me very sad indeed.

A short time after this a fellow cab-horse told me he had heard that a horse from Ginger's stable had died while pulling too heavy a load. I never learned any more about the incident but I did hear that the horse was a chestnut with a long thin neck, and that it had a white streak down the forehead. No-one knew his name. I believe it was Ginger; I hoped it was, for then her troubles would be over. Oh, if only men were more merciful, they would shoot us before we came to such misery.

* * * * *

Christmas and the New Year are very merry times for some people, but for cabmen and cabmen's horses it is no holiday, though it may be a harvest. There are so many parties, balls, and places of amusement open, that the work is hard and often late. Sometimes driver and horse have to wait for hours in the rain or frost, shivering with cold, whilst the merry people within are dancing away to the music. I wonder if the beautiful

[183]

ladies ever think of the weary cabman waiting on his box, and his patient beast standing till his legs get stiff with cold.

I had most of the evening work, as I was well accustomed to standing, and Jerry was also more afraid of Captain taking cold. We had a great deal of late work in the Christmas week, and Jerry's cough was bad, but however late we were, Polly sat up for him, and came out with the lantern to meet him, looking anxious and troubled.

On the evening of the New Year, we had to take two gentlemen to a house in one of the West End squares. We set them down at nine o'clock and were told to come again at eleven. 'But,' said one of them, 'as it is a card party, you may have to wait a few minutes, but don't be late.'

As the clock struck eleven we were at the door, for Jerry was always punctual. The clock chimed the quarters — one, two, three, and then struck twelve, but the door did not open.

The wind had been very changeable, with squalls of rain during the day, but now it came on a sharp driving sleet, which seemed to come all the way round; it was very cold and there was no shelter. Jerry got off his box and came and pulled one of my cloths a little more over my neck; then he took a turn or two up and down, stamping his feet; then he began to beat his arms, but that set him off coughing, so he opened the cab door and sat at the bottom with his feet on the pavement, and was a little sheltered. Still the clock chimed the quarters, and no one came. At half-past twelve, he rang the bell and asked the servant if he would be wanted that night.

'Oh, yes, you'll be wanted safe enough,' said the man, 'you must not go, it will soon be over,' and again Jerry sat down, but his voice was so hoarse I could hardly hear him.

At a quarter past one the door opened, and the two gentle-

And it came down pouring

men came out. They got into the cab without a word, and told Jerry where to drive — that was nearly two miles. My legs were numbed with cold, and I thought I should have stumbled. When the men got out, they never said they were sorry to have kept us waiting so long, but were angry at the charge.

At last we got home. Jerry could hardly speak, and his cough was dreadful. Polly asked no questions, but opened the door and held the lantern for him.

'Can't I do something?' she said.

'Yes, get Jack something warm, and then boil me some gruel.'

This was said in a hoarse whisper; he could hardly get his breath, but he gave me a rub down as usual, and even went up into the hayloft for an extra bundle of straw for my bed. Polly brought me a warm mash that made me comfortable, and then locked the door.

It was late the next morning before anyone came, and then it was only Harry. He cleaned us and fed us, and swept out the stalls. Then he put the straw back again as if it was Sunday. He was very still, and neither whistled nor sang. At noon he came again and gave us our food and water. This time Dolly came with him. She was crying, and I could gather from what they said that Jerry was dangerously ill, and the doctor said it was a bad case. So two days passed, and there was great trouble indoors.

Jerry grew better slowly, but the doctor said that he must never go back to the cab-work again if he wished to be an old man. The children had many consultations together about what Father and Mother would do, and how they could help to earn money.

It was settled in the end that as soon as Jerry was well enough they should remove to the country, and that the cab and horses should be sold as soon as possible.

This was heavy news for me, for I was not young now, and could not look for any improvement in my condition. Since I left Birtwick I had never been so happy as with my dear master, Jerry; but three years of cab-work, even under the best conditions, will tell on one's strength, and I felt that I was not the horse that I had been.

* * * * *

I shall never forget my new master. He had black eyes and a hook nose, his mouth was as full of teeth as a bulldog's, and his voice was as harsh as the grinding of cart wheels over gravel stones. His name was Nicholas Skinner.

I have heard men say that seeing is believing, but I should say that feeling is believing for, much as I had seen before, I never knew till now the utter misery of a cab-horse's life.

Skinner had a low set of cabs and a low set of drivers. He was hard on the men, and the men were hard on the horses. In this place we had no Sunday rest, and it was in the heat of summer.

My life was now so utterly wretched that I wished I might, like Ginger, drop down dead at my work, and be out of my misery for ever, and one day my wish very nearly came to pass.

I went on the stand at eight in the morning, and had done a good share of work, when we had to take a fare to the railway. A long train was just expected in, so my driver pulled up at the back of some of the outside cabs, to take the chance of a return fare. It was a very heavy train, and as all the cabs were soon engaged, ours was called for. There was a party of four; a noisy, blustering man with a lady, a little boy, and a young girl, and a great deal of luggage. The lady and the boy got into the cab, and while the man ordered about the luggage, the young girl came and looked at me.

'Papa', she said, 'I am sure this poor horse cannot take us and all our luggage so far. He is so very weak and worn out; do look at him.'

'Oh! he's all right, miss,' said my driver. 'He's strong enough.'

The porter, who was pulling about some heavy boxes, suggested to the gentleman, as there was so much luggage, that it might be as well to take a second cab.

'Can your horse do it, or can't he?' said the blustering man.

'Papa, I'm sure this poor horse can't take us and all our luggage!'

'Oh, he can do it all right, sir. Send up the boxes, porter;
he could take more than that,' and he helped to haul up a box
so heavy that I could feel the springs go down. Box after box
was dragged up and lodged on the top of the cab, or settled
by the side of the driver. At last all was ready, and with his
usual jerk at the rein, and slash of the whip, he drove me out
of the station.

The load was very heavy, and I had had neither food nor
rest since the morning; but I did my best, as I always had done,
in spite of cruelty and injustice.

I got along fairly till we came to Ludgate Hill, but there
the heavy load and my own exhaustion were too much. I was
struggling to keep on, goaded by constant chucks of the rein

[188]

and use of the whip, when, in a single moment — I cannot tell how — my feet slipped from under me, and I fell heavily to the ground on my side. The suddenness and the force with which I fell seemed to beat all the breath out of my body. I lay perfectly still; indeed, I had not power to move, and I thought now I was going to die. I heard a sort of confusion round me, loud angry voices, and the getting down of the luggage, but it was all like a dream. I thought I heard that sweet pitiful voice saying, 'Oh, that poor horse! It is all our fault.' Someone came and loosened the throat strap of my bridle, and undid the traces which kept the collar so tight upon me. Someone said, 'He's dead, he'll never get up again.' Then I could hear a policeman giving orders, but I did not even open my eyes, I could only draw a gasping breath now and then. Some cold water was thrown over my head, and some cordial was poured into my mouth, and a cover or something was put over me. I know not how long I lay there, but I found my life coming back, and a kind-voiced man was patting me and encouraging me to rise. After some more cordial had been given me, and after one or two attempts, I staggered to my feet, and was gently led to some stables close by. Here I was put into a well-littered stall, and some warm gruel was brought to me, which I drank thankfully.

In the evening I was sufficiently recovered to be led back to Skinner's stables, where I think they did the best for me they could. In the morning Skinner came with a farrier to look at me. He examined me very closely, and said:

'This is a case of overwork more than disease, and if you could give him a run off for six months, he would be able to work again; but now there is not an ounce of strength in him.'

'Then he must go to the dogs,' said Skinner; 'I have no

meadows to nurse sick horses in — he might get well or he might not. That sort of thing don't suit my business. My plan is to work 'em as long as they'll go, and then sell 'em for what they'll fetch at the knacker's or elsewhere.'

'If he was broken-winded,' said the farrier, 'you had better have him killed out of hand, but he is not. There is a sale of horses coming off in about ten days. If you rest him and feed him up, he may pick up, and you may get more than his skin is worth, anyway.'

Upon this advice, Skinner, rather unwillingly, I think, gave orders that I should be well fed and cared for, and the stable man, happily for me, carried out the orders with a much better will than his master had in giving them. Ten days of perfect rest, plenty of good oats, hay, bran mashes, with boiled linseed mixed in them, did more to get up my condition than anything else could have done. Those linseed mashes were delicious, and I began to think, after all, it might be better to live than go to the dogs. When the twelfth day after the accident came, I was taken to the sale, a few miles out of London. I felt that any change from my present place must be an improvement, so I held up my head, and hoped for the best.

*　*　*　*　*

At this sale, of course, I found myself in company with the broken-down horses — some lame, some broken-winded, some old, and some that I am sure it would have been merciful to shoot. Coming from the better part of the fair, I noticed a man who looked like a gentleman farmer, with a young boy by his side. He had a broad back and round shoulders, a kind, ruddy face, and he wore a broad-brimmed hat. I saw his eye rest on me. I had still a good mane and tail, which did something for my appearance. I pricked my ears and looked at him.

'There's a horse, Willie, that has known better days.'

'Poor old fellow!' said the boy, 'do you think, Grandpapa, he was ever a carriage horse?'

'Oh yes, my boy,' said the farmer, 'he might have been anything when he was young. Look at his nostrils and his ears, the shape of his neck and shoulder; there's a deal of breeding about that horse.' He gave me a kind pat on the neck. I put out my nose in answer to his kindness. The boy stroked my face.

'Poor old fellow! See, Grandpapa, how well he understands kindness. Could you not buy him for the ladies? He would be just right for them.'

'What is the lowest you will take for him?' said the farmer to Skinner's man.

'Five pounds, sir. That was the lowest price my master set.'

'It's a speculation,' said the old gentleman, shaking his head, but at the same time slowly drawing out his purse — 'quite a speculation!' he said, counting the sovereigns into his hand.

'If the ladies take to him,' said the old gentleman, 'they'll be suited, and he'll be suited; we can but try.'

I was led home, placed in a comfortable stable, fed, and left to myself. The next day, when my groom was cleaning my face, he said:

'That is just like the star that Black Beauty had, he is much the same height too. I wonder where he is now.'

'White star on the forehead, one white foot on the off side, this little knot just in that place'; then looking at the middle of my back — 'and as I am alive, there is that little patch of white hair that John used to call "Beauty's three-penny bit".

It must be Black Beauty! Why, Beauty! Beauty! do you know me? Little Joe Green, that almost killed you?' And he began patting me as if he was quite overjoyed.

I could not say that I remembered him, for now he was a fine-grown young fellow, with black whiskers and a man's voice, but I was sure he knew me, and that he was Joe Green, and I was very glad. I put my nose up to him, and tried to say that we were friends. I never saw a man so pleased.

'Give you a fair trial! I should think so indeed! I wonder who the rascal was that broke your knees, my old Beauty! You must have been badly scrved out somewhere. Well, well, it won't be my fault if you haven't good times of it now.'

In the afternoon I was put into a low Park chair and brought to the door. Miss Ellen was going to try me, and Green went with her. I soon found that she was a good driver, and she seemed pleased with my paces. I heard Joe telling her about me, and that he was sure I was Squire Gordon's old Black Beauty.

When we returned, the other sisters came out to hear how I had behaved myself. She told them what she had just heard, and said:

'I shall certainly write to Mrs. Gordon, and tell her that her favourite horse has come to us. How pleased she will be!'

After this I was driven every day for a week or so, and as I appeared to be quite safe, Miss Lavinia at last ventured out in the small closed carriage. It was quite decided to keep me, and call me by my old name of 'Black Beauty'.

WITHDRAWN

BY
WILLIAMSBURG REGIONAL LIBRARY